Jack Fortune

and the Search for the Hidden Valley

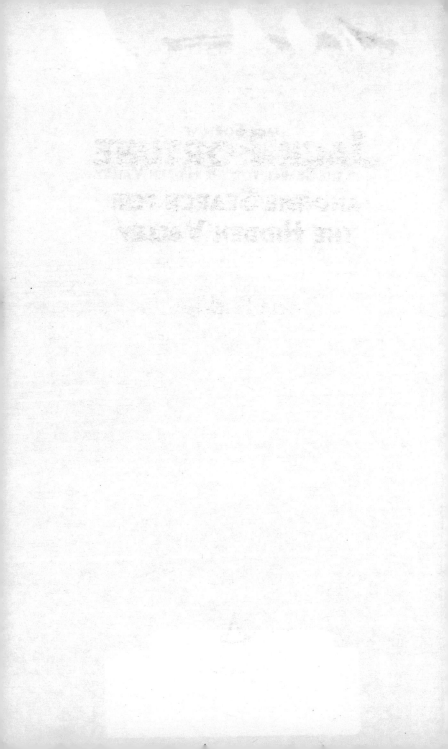

JACK FORTUNE
AND THE SEARCH FOR THE HIDDEN VALLEY

Sue Purkiss

ALMA BOOKS

ALMA BOOKS LTD
3 Castle Yard
Richmond
Surrey TW10 6TF
United Kingdom
www.almajunior.com

Jack Fortune and the Search for the Hidden Valley first published by
Alma Books Ltd in 2017

© Sue Purkiss, 2017

Sue Purkiss asserts her moral right to be identified as the author of this
work in accordance with the Copyright, Designs and Patents Act 1988

Printed in Great Britain by CPI Group (UK) Ltd, Croydon CR0 4YY

ISBN: 978-1-84688-428-3

THIS BOOK IS FOR MY PARENTS,
WHO PUT SO MUCH LOVE
INTO THEIR GARDENING.

would venture to say that I have probably heard it all before."

Lady Smythe darted a look of fury at Jack, and said, "Oh no, Mrs Greville – I don't think you've heard anything quite like *this* before. Whilst I was attending to arrangements for tea, *that boy* persuaded my darling Cecily to play a game called 'Sardines'. Perhaps you know it? One child hides, then, as the other children find her, they hide in the same place. By the time the bell was rung for tea, there wasn't a child to be seen. We searched the house from top to bottom. I was most *fearfully* worried. Can you guess where we eventually found them, Mrs Greville?"

Jack really was feeling *very* sick.

"I fear I cannot," said his aunt, twisting his ear painfully. "Please enlighten me."

He didn't think he could hold it in much longer...

"In the cellar!" declared Her Ladyship, her eyes flashing with anger. "Between them they had drunk a whole bottle of sherry and started on His Lordship's best port. Can you *imagine* the state they were in? Can you conceive of my feelings, Mrs Greville, as a mother and a hostess? Can you picture my distress? Never, never in my entire life..."

...Oh, he did feel bad. He'd never, ever felt this bad. His stomach was heaving and there was a horrible taste in his mouth. No – it was no use – he just couldn't hold it in any longer! He pitched forward, opened his mouth – and sprayed the contents of his stomach all over Aunt Constance's best Wilton carpet, the hem of her lavender silk dress and the toes of her fine kid shoes...

CHAPTER TWO

Aunt Constance Draws the Line

Jack hovered anxiously in the drawing room. Four days had passed since the party, and Aunt Constance hadn't said a word to him. That wasn't a problem – in fact it was really rather pleasant – but it was a clear sign that trouble was brewing. Then last night Uncle Edmund had arrived. He only ever came at Christmas, so this was decidedly odd – it was the end of January now. Why was he here again so soon? And at breakfast that morning, Aunt Constance had told Sarah to light the fire in the library. She only ever used the library for significant discussions. These were usually about Jack and tended to be followed very swiftly by disagreeable consequences. Trouble was definitely afoot and heading his way.

Jack glanced casually around. No one was about, so he slipped out of the drawing room, across the hall and into the library. A sofa faced the fireplace, and beside it was a round table on which stood a large plant in a blue-and-white china pot.

The table was covered by a thick red chenille cloth with a fringed edge which fell to the floor. Jack knew it was an excellent place to hide because he'd used it before. He crawled under the table and tried to get comfortable. Surely it hadn't been this cramped last time? He must have grown. He drew his knees up to his chest, clasped his hands around them, ducked his head and settled down to wait.

Fortunately, it wasn't long before he heard voices.

"Come, Edmund – don't dally!" snapped Aunt Constance. "We have serious matters to discuss."

And off she went, droning on and on about Cecily's stupid party and how furious Lady Smythe had been and how she'd probably never ask Aunt Constance to tea ever again. Although his uncle made a few half-hearted attempts, it was ages before he could even get a word in.

"My dear Connie," he said cautiously, "I sympathize with your difficulties, I truly do. But…"

"*My* difficulties? You seem to forget, Edmund, as you so often do, that Jack is *your* nephew too!"

Jack heard Uncle Edmund gulp. "I haven't forgotten. But as we know, our dear Annamaria chose to leave him in your care – and quite rightly so.

You're making a splendid job of it, Connie. Really marvellous!"

"Oh no I'm not," fired back Aunt Constance. "Haven't you listened to a word I've said? Jack's out of control. It's all too clear whom he takes after – he's every bit as ungovernable as that dreadful father of his. Oh, if only my dear husband were still alive! He wouldn't put up with such behaviour for an *instant*. It's just one thing after another – you simply can't imagine!"

"Oh, I think I can. After all, I was a boy once too."

"Not one like Jack!"

Ouch! Jack winced. But worse was to come. Off she went again. He was quite shocked – she certainly knew how to bear a grudge. She told one story after another, starting with the frogs Jack had smuggled into one of her tea parties (oh, that had been fun!), going on to the magnificent dam he and Will built, which dried up the water supply for Farmer Barker's cattle, and finishing up with the peaches episode. Jack was still sore about that. It had been last summer. He had been locked in his room simply for picking some peaches. He thought it was most unfair. How was he supposed to know that the gardener had been bringing them on for weeks so they'd be perfectly ripe on the exact night the Duke and Duchess of Rochester were coming to supper? It wasn't fair, and he had decided to escape by climbing down the ivy. Everything went well until he dislodged a tile, which unfortunately crashed into the greenhouse. Shards of glass went flying, and one of them only just missed the Reverend Prout, Jack's tutor, who had come to report on his pupil's lack of progress.

The list went on and on. Aunt Constance's voice rose higher and higher. She was becoming quite hysterical, and Uncle Edmund tried to calm her down.

It wouldn't work. Jack could have told him that.

"I'll certainly have a word, Connie, but—"

"A word?" she cried. "A *word*? Oh no, Edmund, oh dear me no. It's gone far beyond words. What's needed is action. And *will* you stop calling me Connie – you know perfectly well I hate it!"

It was hot and cramped under the heavy tablecloth. Jack was very uncomfortable, but he told himself that it was all good training. He and Will were going to be explorers when they grew up. They had it all planned. They were going to explore mountains and deserts and distant oceans, and the great southern continent which Captain Cook had discovered on the other side of the world, only a few years ago in 1768. Obviously, he would have to put up with extremes of heat and cold, so he might as well get used to it... hang on – Uncle Edmund was saying something. He sounded a lot closer – sensible chap, he must be trying to put some distance between himself and Aunt Constance.

"What about sending him away to school?" said Uncle Edmund.

What? Jack was horrified. He had heard about school. School meant rules and punishments and bad food. It meant being shut in and shut up and told what to do. No, he wasn't having that.

"I believe there are many excellent boarding schools these days – just the thing for a boy like Jack. There now – I think that's a splendid solution to your problem!"

How *could* he? Jack could hardly believe it. He'd always thought Uncle Edmund was a fairly decent sort – a bit wet, but basically harmless. But this was completely out of order.

"Our problem, Edmund – *our* problem," said Aunt Constance, her voice dripping acid. "I can't send Jack away to school because, as I'm sure you will recall if you'll only take the trouble to think for a moment, I made a solemn promise to his mother that I never would. She thought schools were dreadful, fierce places – quite unsuitable for her dear child."

"Yes," said Uncle Edmund, adding – very rudely, Jack thought: "but she didn't know that her dear child was going to turn into Jack, did she?"

"Nevertheless," said Aunt Constance, "a promise is a promise. And Annamaria may have been the silliest girl on earth, but she *was* my sister."

At that, Jack was furious. She could insult his father, she could insult Jack himself – and did, often – but his mother? No – that was simply not on. Quite forgetting that he was under a table, he leapt up, determined to come to the defence of his beloved parent.

Disaster struck.

His fingers caught in the fringe of the tablecloth. The table tipped over, the cloth stayed with Jack, and the aspidistra flew up into the air before coming down to land. The bowl smashed to smithereens and soil flew everywhere.

Jack knew he didn't have much time. "Aunt Constance," he announced, adjusting the tablecloth round his shoulders with dignity, "I'm afraid I really cannot allow you to say things like that about my mother."

Aunt Constance's eyes narrowed and Jack backed away a little.

"That bowl," she hissed, "was Ming Dynasty. It was my dear husband's last gift to me, before he left on that ill-fated voyage to Virginia. It was worth more money than you can possibly imagine. Every time I think you've gone too far, you somehow manage to go just that little bit further. Jack Fortune, go to your room this instant – and STAY THERE!"

Clearly, she was beyond all reason. Jack cast off the tablecloth and marched out of the room and up the stairs, passing Mrs Stewart the housekeeper and Sarah the housemaid. They had come scurrying when they heard all the noise. Mrs Stewart glared at Jack, but Sarah winked at him.

When he reached the landing, Jack ducked down behind the banister and peeked through the railings to see what would happen next. The library door was open, and Mrs Stewart and Sarah were bustling in and out with dustpans. Jack could see his uncle fiddling with ornaments on the mantelpiece. His back was turned to Aunt Constance, who was supervising the cleaning-up. His shoulders were shaking slightly – most likely in fear, Jack thought. Well, Uncle Edmund needn't come to him for sympathy. School, indeed!

Once the mess had been cleared up, Aunt Constance ushered Sarah and Mrs Stewart out of the room, glared up towards Jack's room, where she supposed he was, then marched back inside and slammed the door.

The coast clear, Jack crept back down and applied his ear to the keyhole.

"*Now* do you see?" his aunt boomed. "I've done my best, no one can say I haven't. But that's it. I can do no more. I – draw – the – line. He's your responsibility now, Edmund. He must come and live with *you*."

"Oh no," said Uncle Edmund hastily, "absolutely not. I'm afraid that's quite out of the question."

"Perhaps you would care to tell me why?" said Aunt Constance icily.

There was a pause. Uncle Edmund cleared his throat. "Well, the fact is… the fact is, that I'm not going to be living in this country for a while. In fact, for the foreseeable future, I'm not going to be living anywhere at all."

"That's an absurd statement, Edmund, even for you. You must be going to live somewhere – everyone has to live *somewhere*!"

She had a point, Jack had to admit.

"What I mean is, I'll be travelling. I'm leaving the country – going a long way away – and I expect to be gone for some considerable time."

Leaving the country? Quiet old Uncle Edmund? Well, that was a surprise!

"*You*? Going abroad? Don't be ridiculous! You *never* go abroad. You wouldn't know *how* to go abroad!"

"A person can change, Constance," said Uncle Edmund stiffly. "It would be a sad world if he could not. I don't believe you know me quite as well as you think you do."

"Oh? Then perhaps you would care to enlighten me. Come, Edmund, tell me: what has led you to change the habits of a lifetime?"

When his uncle answered, Jack could tell by his voice that he had moved farther away.

"You have a pretty garden, Constance," he was saying. Ah, he must be by the window. "Full of all the old familiar plants. Roses, lavender… a holly bush by the gate and box hedges along the path. But isn't that a magnolia in the centre of the lawn?"

Why on earth was he talking about *plants*?

"Yes, of course it is," said Aunt Constance impatiently. "What of it? Don't change the subject!"

"Just bear with me a moment, if you wouldn't mind. Now, where do you think that tree came from?"

"I haven't the faintest idea," snapped Aunt Constance. "It's *always* been there. If you have a point, Edmund – which, frankly, I've always doubted – please get to it."

"Ah," said Uncle Edmund triumphantly, "that's where you're wrong. It hasn't always been there. Until something over a century ago, there were no magnolias in Britain at all, not one. A man called John Tradescant brought the seeds of the first one from America. Just think of it – if he hadn't set off to explore that wild and savage continent, there would *still* be none!"

"I'm losing patience," warned Aunt Constance. "If you don't start making sense within the next thirty seconds, I fear I shall begin throwing things. This paperweight, for instance!"

"Oh, right. Well," said Uncle Edmund hastily, "the point is that Tradescant was a naturalist, just like me. Only he wasn't content to potter about close to home, he—"

"Just like *you*?"

"Well, really, I don't know why you say it like that. I've always been interested in natural science – you know I have – even as a boy."

"What – you mean all those boxes of birds' eggs and butterflies with pins in?"

"Yes, all that and much more," said Uncle Edmund huffily. "You may not be aware of it, but my monograph on the reproductive system of field mushrooms has attracted a great deal of very favourable attention. And now, like Tradescant, I'm going to take my work a step further. I'm going to travel to faraway lands in search of plants which we in the West have never before set eyes on. I am going to the far north of India – to a place of snow-topped mountains and steamy jungles – in short, to the kingdom of Hakkim!"

Jack swallowed, his mouth suddenly dry. Could this possibly be true? Was dopey old Uncle Edmund really about to do such an incredibly splendid thing? And if he was – could Jack somehow wangle it so he could go too?

A pause. Then, in a voice as cold as ice: "In that case, my dear Edmund, you will simply have to take Jack with you."

Jack gasped. Had she really said that? Oh, bless her! Bless dear, darling Aunt Constance!

"But Connie – haven't you listened to a word I've said? Where I'm going is unknown territory. There could be fierce animals – poisonous snakes – hostile people! It's *far* too dangerous for a child!"

Jack hopped from one foot to the other. Perhaps he should go and join in the discussion? He couldn't miss this chance – he just couldn't. In all the times he and Will had talked about their future careers as explorers, he'd never once imagined that he'd be able to make a start so soon. What was she saying now?

"Believe me, it'll be far more dangerous if you try to leave him here. For you, I mean. And, for the last time, do *not* call me Connie!"

"What? Now then, Con… steady on. Don't do anything you'll—"

There was a tremendous crash, followed by the sound of feet running towards the door. Jack leapt back, just in time for Uncle Edmund to burst out of the library, slamming the door behind him. Something smashed against it with terrifying force. Uncle Edmund, wild-eyed and white-faced, met Jack's gaze.

"Enemy behind, Jack – no time to lose! RUN FOR IT!"

Over the next few days, the discussion raged on. But Aunt Constance would not change her mind. When Uncle Edmund left, he would take Jack with him, and that was that.

Jack could see that his uncle didn't quite appreciate what a brilliant idea this was, but he was sure he'd come round to it. After all, Uncle Edmund had never hacked his way through undergrowth, or climbed a tree to get his bearings, or set traps in the woods, whereas Jack and Will did this kind of thing all the time. No, there was no doubt about it – Uncle Edmund *needed* him.

Almost as much, in fact, as Jack needed Uncle Edmund.

CHAPTER THREE

London

On the whole, Jack was perfectly happy about leaving Little Stinchcombe. He certainly wouldn't miss Aunt Constance.

But he would miss Will. Will was the son of the village blacksmith, and he had lots of brothers and sisters – Sarah, the housemaid at Coombe Lodge, was one of them. Jack loved the warmth and cheerfulness of their crowded, noisy cottage. Sometimes he even pretended to himself that he was one of the family. Oh yes, he would certainly miss Will.

Before he left, the two of them went on one last expedition into the woods. They made a solemn toast with the inch of sherry left in a bottle that Jack had liberated from the glass-fronted cabinet at Coombe Lodge.

"To the expedition!" said Will generously.

Jack felt awful. "I wish you could come too," he said.

Will shrugged. "Can't be helped," he said bravely. "India, though. Hot there, isn't it?"

Jack considered. He had tried to find out more about the expedition from Uncle Edmund, but his uncle had been very glum since the episode in the library, and it had been difficult to get much out of him.

"Think so. But Uncle says the bit we're going to is in the north. There are mountains, really big ones, so there'll be snow and ice as well."

Will nodded enviously. "That'll be amazing. Anyway – you'll tell me all about it when you come back?"

"Course."

"How long will you be away?"

Jack shook his head. "Don't know. Shouldn't think we'll be back by Christmas, though."

Will looked gloomy, and Jack tried to think of some way to cheer him up. "Shall we dig the rat up again?"

That did the trick.

Sarah gave him a package the evening before he left, and when he opened it he found a long, warm scarf.

"I was knitting it for Father, for his birthday," she explained, "but our Will said it might be cold where you're going, so I thought I'd give it to you instead. I'll knit another one for him." Then she bent down and hugged him. "Take care, young Jack. Be good and do as you're told. And see you come back safe."

Jack blinked, and told himself, very firmly, that explorers never cry.

It was a long journey from Little Stinchcombe to London, but they were the only ones in the public coach, so they were able to make themselves comfortable. Jack seized the opportunity to find out more about their expedition.

"We'll be proper explorers, Uncle, won't we?" he said. "I expect it'll be very dangerous. Will there be wild animals?"

Uncle Edmund looked a little worried. "I suppose there will be. But I don't know what kind. Very few travellers from the West have been to Hakkim – it's very remote."

"Where is it again?" asked Jack. Geography had never been a strong point of his.

"It's in the foothills of the Himalayas – quite a small country."

Foothills? Jack was disappointed – that didn't sound very dramatic. "I expect there'll be jungles, though?" he said hopefully.

"Yes, indeed. That's one reason why I want to go there, Jack. There are not many places where tropical plants grow in such close proximity to plants which would be happy in the icy cold of the Arctic. I hope to study the growth patterns, you see, so that I can discover to what extent the *place* where plants grow has a bearing on *how* they grow..."

Jack yawned loudly, and his eyes began to glaze over, but Uncle Edmund didn't notice.

"And there's something else." He gazed out of the window, and his voice softened. "You see, Jack, it is my greatest hope that one day I might be noticed by Sir Joseph Banks, the director of Kew Botanical Gardens. He is a member of the Royal Society, a confidant of King George himself! Oh, these are exciting times for scientists, Jack, make no mistake... and if I can return from the Himalayas with something special – why, who knows what might become possible!

"There is a particular plant I have in mind. We know that there, in Hakkim, there are rhododendrons of every shade. Every shade, that is, except blue. If I could only manage to find a blue one, Jack – why, that could change everything. It could make my fortune!"

He turned to his nephew, a smile on his face. But Jack had dozed off, and Edmund's smile faded.

The expedition was not without risk: there would be a long voyage by sea, then a journey overland – even before he ventured into the little-known country of Hakkim. He might encounter all sorts of dangers. He had accepted that. But he hadn't planned on Jack tagging along. The stakes had suddenly got a good deal higher, and the rules of the game might have to change. He would risk his own life if necessary, but he couldn't risk Jack's. He looked at his sleeping nephew and sighed. Jack was a complication he could have done without.

Jack pressed his nose against the window in the library, staring at his uncle as he disappeared down the street. Things were not working out quite as he'd hoped. It had been a week since he'd arrived at Uncle Edmund's house, but he had yet to go out of the front door. He'd thought London would be exciting, but so far it was no fun at all.

Out there in the city all manner of things must be going on. That boy across the road, for instance. There he was, just strolling along all by himself, his blue cap tipped at a jaunty angle, without a care in the world. *He* didn't have to stay indoors and twiddle his thumbs. It was such a stupid waste. Jack could be such a help to Uncle Edmund, what with all his practical experience. When was the last time Uncle Edmund had sneaked out of the house after dark and camped under the stars in the woods, making a fire and eating delicious slices of burnt bacon? What did *he* know about setting traps and living off the land?

He wondered what Will was doing now. Having a lot more fun than him, that was for sure. There was nothing to do, absolutely nothing. He'd pointed this out to Uncle Edmund that morning at breakfast, and his uncle had looked at him, then taken him into the library and waved an arm at all the books.

"Nothing to do, Jack? Nothing to do? There's a whole world to discover between the covers of those books. History, philosophy, science, poetry – what could possibly be more exciting?"

Jack took one of the books his uncle handed him. He wrinkled his nose. It smelt musty and old. He leafed through it. The print was very small, and there were no pictures.

"Have you got any stories?" he asked, without much hope.

"Stories? What, made-up things? Well – no, I hardly think so," said Uncle Edmund. "Why would you need stories, with all this wealth of knowledge at your fingertips?"

Then he'd snapped open his pocket watch and said he must be off. There was much to do before they embarked, and he had simply no idea how he was going to manage it all.

"But I could help," Jack offered yet again. "Why won't you let me?"

His uncle began to edge away. "Oh no. I don't think so. I'll just… get on. Yes, that's definitely the best thing. I'll see you later, Jack. Enjoy your reading," he called back over his shoulder as he made a hasty exit.

Jack breathed a cloud of mist onto the window pane and drew a pattern on it with his finger. It was so unfair… then his eyes narrowed. The boy in the blue cap was talking to an old gentleman. The old man was bending down, as if he couldn't hear very well. The boy suddenly tapped him on the shoulder and pointed. The old man straightened up and twisted round to look – and in an instant, the boy's hand flashed out and filched something from his coat pocket. The old man let out a cry, but it was too late – the boy was off, lost in the crowd.

Jack was outraged. He wasn't going to stand by and let that happen. He dashed out of the library and along the hall, wrenched open the heavy front door, ran down the steps and onto the street and gave chase, dimly hearing startled shouts behind him.

He darted through the crowd, using his elbows to push his way through, ignoring the angry cries. He spotted the blue cap – it was some way ahead of him, but Jack was a fast runner, and he soon began to catch up.

"Hey, you!" he shouted. "Blue hat! Yes, you!"

The boy looked round in surprise. Then he took off with Jack after him.

The boy twisted and turned, and soon Jack found himself in a part of London he didn't know at all. The streets were narrow and dark, and close-packed houses with dirty windows crowded in on him. The well-dressed crowds had dwindled and finally disappeared, and he'd lost sight of the boy. He must have ducked into a doorway. Jack stopped and looked around uncertainly. What should he do now? Then the boy sauntered out in front of him, his thumbs stuck in his belt.

"Bit out of yer way, aren't yer?" he asked.

"You stole something from that old man," accused Jack. The boy was smaller than him. If it came to a fight, Jack felt sure he could win. "Give it back!"

"Why? It ain't yourn, is it?"

"Bit of a nosy parker is he, your new pal? Now then, we can't have that, can we?" It was a man's voice, and it came from behind him. Jack whirled, but as he did so, something dark and rough came down over his head. Pain exploded in his head, and his knees buckled under him.

Jack stirred. His head was throbbing, and it hurt when he moved it. His eyelids fluttered open, and he saw his uncle's face hanging over him.

"Jack! Oh, thank goodness you're all right! Here, let me help you to sit up."

Jack blinked. He was lying on his bed in his room at Uncle Edmund's house. He thought back groggily.

"What happened?" he said.

"You ran away, for what reason I cannot think. Fortunately, you were spotted by George, my footman. By all accounts you led him a merry chase, and he finally caught up with you in Butcher's Market, just as you were being set on by a couple of ruffians. Luckily, George is an enthusiastic boxer – so he tells me – and he was able to see them off and bring you home. You have him to thank for your escape."

George was standing at the foot of the bed. Jack managed to smile at him, and George grinned and gave him a large wink.

"But what were you thinking of, Jack? The streets of London are not safe for those who do not understand their dangers – I dread to think what might have happened to you. Think what your Aunt Constance would have said! I really cannot put up with this kind of behaviour – you must give me your absolute word that there will be no more such escapades."

"But Uncle, I was only trying to help—"

"I don't want to hear it! Aunt Constance was right, Jack. You really are a danger, both to yourself and others. From now on, I must absolutely insist that you do not leave this house, except to go into the garden. And I will ask George to ensure that you don't."

Jack was furious. Aunt Constance had been a dragon, but at least she hadn't kept him prisoner – well, not often, and not for long.

He was beginning to wish he'd never left Little Stinchcombe.

The next day, though, he felt much better, with only a large lump on the side of his head to remind him of his adventure. Mrs Austen, the housekeeper, had decreed that he must stay in bed at least for the morning, but although it was fun to have breakfast in bed for once, he wasn't planning on going back to sleep. He looked round the room for something to do, and spotted his father's old painting bag on a hook on the back of the door. Apart from his clothes, it was the only familiar object in the room. He took it everywhere with him.

He got out of bed and padded over to fetch it. It was a good-sized soft-leather satchel, battered and well used, with a set of initials – $\mathcal{MPF}$ – tooled into the flap. When Jack was little, he hadn't realized they were letters. He'd thought they were just a pattern, with their loops and curls. He used to copy them, and then one day Aunt Constance noticed what he was doing and said the letters were his father's initials, standing for Matthew Percival Fortune. She said she supposed he ought to know, as the bag was the only thing his useless father had managed to leave him.

Jack traced the letters with his finger, carefully following the intricate loops. It was something he did when he needed to think. It helped him to concentrate. Then he opened the bag and took out his father's paintbox and sketchbook.

He couldn't remember his parents at all. They'd died when he was very small. Aunt Constance seldom spoke of them – she said she found it too upsetting – but Will's mother had been a maid at Coombe Lodge when Aunt Constance, Edmund and Annamaria had been young, and she had filled in some of the gaps.

Jack's father had been an illustrator. He'd met Jack's mother when he was employed to give her drawing lessons. They had fallen very much in love, Will's mother used to tell him, dabbing her eyes with a corner of her apron; anyone could see they were meant for each other. But Matthew Fortune, contrary to his name, had no money, and Annamaria's parents wouldn't hear of a match. Annamaria refused to give Matthew up, so she defied her family and ran away with him. They married, were blissfully happy and eventually made a kind of peace with Annamaria's family.

Then one day Matthew had to go to Venice to do some illustrations for a long poem about a princess and a pirate. He took Annamaria with him. By now they had a baby – Jack. He was too small to travel, so they left him in the care of Aunt Constance and his grandparents. Venice was a low-lying city, an unhealthy place criss-crossed by canals and surrounded by marshes. Matthew caught a deadly fever. Annamaria nursed him devotedly, caught the fever from him and they both died. (By this stage in the story, Will's mother's apron was usually wet through.)

Jack had never been able to forgive his father for this. It was quite clearly all his fault. Why did he have to insist on going to Venice? It was a stupid poem anyway – Jack had searched it out and read it. And if he did choose to go, why hadn't he left Annamaria at home with Jack? If he hadn't been so selfish and careless, both of them would still be alive. They would have been happy, the three of them together, and Aunt Constance would be just an old battleaxe they had to visit once or twice a year.

Jack flipped through what must have been his father's last sketchbook, with the pictures he'd done of Venice, all carefully labelled. Then he came to his favourite picture, the one he specially loved.

It showed a woman's face. Her head was thrown back, and she was laughing. Her hair was curly like Jack's, and tendrils flew around her face like springy gold wire. Her eyes were dark, like Uncle Edmund's. She was Jack's mother. At the bottom of the page, his father had written "*Annamaria, mia cara*". Jack gently touched her painted cheek, and told her about the journey to India.

"It *will* be good, I'm sure," he assured her, "but to be honest, it's not much fun at the moment. There's nothing to do. And… and there's nobody to talk to. Uncle Edmund doesn't say much, and I can't understand half of what he *does* say." He did miss Will and Sarah. Even Aunt Constance and Mr Prout had been company of a kind, he thought glumly.

He waited hopefully, as if his mother might somehow find a way to answer him. But she didn't. He stroked her cheek again, and turned the page, but the rest of the book was empty. He looked at it thoughtfully.

Jack had never had the least desire to follow in his father's footsteps. If being a painter meant you abandoned your child, took your wife off to a swampy city and got her killed, he wasn't interested, thank you very much. But there was nothing else to do, so he got dressed, rummaged in the bag for pencils and went out into the garden. He supposed it wouldn't hurt to do some sketching. It wasn't what he was going to do with his life, but it would pass the time.

And it did pass the time. In fact, while he was drawing, the time flew by. There were lots of things to sketch in the garden – trees, a pond with a fountain, a bird perched on a spade. At first, he wasn't satisfied with his pictures and tore them up impatiently, but he kept at it, and gradually they got better. He didn't tell his uncle what he was doing, certain that he wouldn't be interested. Uncle Edmund was much too busy to notice what he got up to, provided he didn't cause any trouble.

At long last, Uncle Edmund announced that everything was ready. He showed Jack some of the equipment he had gathered together – a folding chair cunningly made from wood and canvas, boxes for seeds, a telescope, a compass, several magnifying glasses, sharp knives for taking cuttings, papers for pressing flowers, notebooks and sketchbooks.

Jack picked up one of the sketchbooks. "What are these for?" he asked.

"Why – all the plants I find will need to be sketched, to show what they look like in their native setting. It would be difficult, if not impossible, to bring whole plants home – seeds and cuttings are easier to transport. It will be *most* important to have accurate drawings."

"I didn't know you could draw, Uncle," said Jack.

Uncle Edmund pulled a face. "I'm not very good at it," he said. "but I cannot afford to pay for an artist to accompany us, so I'll just have to do my best. It's a pity you don't seem to have taken after your father, Jack, else you might have proved a very useful member of this expedition."

Jack was silent. He was quite certain he was going to be *extremely* useful – but not as an artist. If his father had been something sensible, instead of an artist, Jack would have two parents now, instead of a cantankerous aunt and an uncle who was, let's face it, a bit feeble. No, he wasn't going to be an artist.

"I will be useful!" he said. "I know heaps about camping, and I can trap things, and climb trees, and I bet I'll be good at climbing mountains too!"

Uncle Edmund looked embarrassed. "Er... yes, Jack, of course. I didn't mean to suggest... I just meant that it would have been *especially* useful if you could draw. Anyway, never mind. The point is, we're ready to go. The day after tomorrow we travel to Southampton, and take ship aboard the HMS *Dauntless*. Oh my goodness – I'm really beginning to feel quite excited!"

Jack was thrilled when he saw the ship they were to travel on. It looked so beautiful with its sails billowing in the breeze and the sun sparkling on the water. He couldn't wait to get to know the sailors – they'd have some stories to tell, for sure. He'd need something to keep him entertained – Uncle Edmund said the voyage would take two months. *Two whole months!* It would be the end of April by the time they reached India. It seemed like for ever.

But Uncle Edmund had other ideas about how Jack was going to fill his time. He declared that the voyage would be an excellent opportunity to improve his education. Jack thought this was a terrible idea, but his uncle was quite determined.

But to Jack's surprise, he found he quite enjoyed the lessons. Uncle Edmund turned out to be a much better teacher than Mr Prout. He told Jack all about the famous explorers – Magellan, Henry the Navigator, Sir Walter Raleigh and, much more recently, Captain Cook, who had explored the great southern continent.

"The world keeps getting bigger, Uncle, doesn't it?" said Jack enthusiastically.

They traced the routes of the great explorers' voyages on maps, and his uncle's eyes lit up as he listed for Jack some of the plants they'd brought back from their travels.

"Strawberries, Jack! Coffee, tea! And potatoes! Where would we be without potatoes, eh?"

And Jack had to admit the world would be a poorer place without roast potatoes and strawberries sprinkled with sugar.

So after two months he knew a lot more about ships and geography, which would be very useful in his future career as an explorer. But when at long last they left the open sea behind, and sailed up the River Hooghly towards Calcutta, he was almost beside himself with excitement: at last their adventure could really begin!

CHAPTER FOUR

Calcutta

Jack stood on deck with Uncle Edmund, watching eagerly as they approached Calcutta. Suddenly there was a deafening bang, and Uncle Edmund almost jumped out of his skin.

"Oh my goodness!" he gasped. "Whatever was that?"

A puff of smoke drifted up into the sky, and Jack smiled.

"It was a cannon, Uncle – that's all!"

"A cannon? We have a cannon? Good Heavens, how terrifying!"

"Oh Uncle – it's just to tell them we're here!"

"Really? Well, it seems a little excessive to me. I should have thought the ship's hooter would suffice. Oh, look, here come some little boats."

"Tugs, Uncle," said Jack. "We had them at Alexandria, do you remember? They pulled us into the harbour."

"Oh yes, so they did. Well done, Jack – you're becoming quite an expert on matters nautical!"

The tugs manoeuvred the big ship slowly in, and Jack hung over the rail. He wanted to take everything in – the exotic-looking boats with their strangely shaped sails, the crowds thronging the quayside, the thick rich scent of salt and spices and food, and the voices calling out in a language he didn't understand – it was all so exciting, so *different*!

As soon as they were moored, Jack hitched his father's bag firmly onto his shoulder, impatient to be off.

"Come on, Uncle – we're here!"

"Yes, I'm aware of that, Jack," said his uncle, looking round distractedly as the passengers began pushing towards the gangplank, "but there's no sense in hurrying – I do detest queueing…"

Jack grinned. "I'm not going to queue!" he called over his shoulder, and he set off to tunnel his way through the crowd.

"Jack, wait!" called his uncle anxiously.

"It's all right, Uncle," he yelled over his shoulder, "I'll see you in India!"

Jack gazed round, enthralled. The quay was crowded with men wearing soft loose clothes and white cloths wound round their heads. It was very warm, and Jack thought that they looked a good deal more comfortable than he felt in his high-collared shirt, itchy wool jacket and tightly buttoned waistcoat. He'd grown during the voyage, so his clothes were really too small, which didn't help. He took off his jacket and slung it over his shoulder, and looked round for his uncle.

"There you are," puffed Uncle Edmund. "My goodness, it's hot, isn't it? Not like spring in England, not a bit. Not that I'd expect it to be, of course… Come on Jack – let's see if we can spot Colonel Kydd."

But it was Colonel Kydd who found them. He and Uncle Edmund had been corresponding for years about plants, and the Colonel had been delighted when he heard that Uncle Edmund was coming to India. They were to stay with him in Calcutta. He was a tall man, rather plump, with several chins, not much hair and a shiny forehead which he mopped constantly. He ushered them into his carriage, and soon they were trotting along a wide street lined with beautiful white buildings, so big they all looked like palaces. Jack was entranced.

Uncle Edmund looked relaxed and happy. "How beautiful it all is! The colours are so bright – oh, look at the blossom on that tree over there! Wonderful!"

"Yes, indeed," said Colonel Kydd. "And you've arrived at the right time of year. The monsoon, now, the rainy season – well, that's quite a different kettle of fish. It simply pours, every day, for weeks and weeks – the plains are covered with floods and travel is quite impossible. But that won't be a problem for you at this time of year – you'll soon be able to travel north to Hakkim." His eyes shone. "Oh, how I envy you! If only my duties permitted, I would have been delighted to accompany you. As you know, Mr Pascoe, botany is my passion. Indeed, I have played a part in establishing the new botanical garden on the west bank of the river, which it would be my very great pleasure to show to you…"

Jack stopped listening and peered out of the coach window. He wanted to take in everything he could see of this city. It was so very different from anywhere he had ever been before.

Jack was surprised by Colonel Kydd's house. It was very comfortable – luxurious even. But the odd thing about it was that, inside, it looked exactly like an English one. Even the pictures looked just like the ones on Aunt Constance's walls. You really wouldn't have known you were in India at all – except for the servants, of course, who looked very different. It seemed odd to Jack.

"What's the point of coming all this way and then living just as if you were at home?" he said to Uncle Edmund on the first evening.

Uncle Edmund looked puzzled. "Why, what else would you expect?" he asked. "We're English. Of course the Colonel would want to live as he would at home."

All the same, later on he put Jack's question to the Colonel, though he wrapped it up much more politely.

"Well, there are those who live as the Indians do. Some even take Indian wives." Then he glanced at Jack and looked embarrassed. "Well, after a fashion, if you take my meaning. And certainly – well, in some ways, it can be good to adapt. Your clothing, for instance – you may find it uncomfortably hot. You might want to have some lighter garments made. I have a tailor who works very quickly."

"Oh, yes please!" said Jack thankfully. That would also solve the problem of his too small clothes. Uncle Edmund smiled, and accepted the Colonel's suggestion.

"I hope you will be able to help us with organizing our onward journey," he said. "I fear I am not even certain as to our mode of transport – will we be able to hire carts?"

"Of course I'll help, my dear fellow – I'm only too delighted to assist a fellow naturalist. The easiest way to travel is by river, as far as you can. You need a special boat for that – the river is very shallow. But that's not a problem – they're easy to hire. Then it'll be horse and cart to Changkot. That's the capital of Hakkim, of course – no carriages there, I'm afraid! And once you're in Hakkim, you'll be on foot – the paths are too narrow and precipitous for horses, even if they had any, which they don't. I'll arrange for the British Resident in

Calcutta to draw up a letter of recommendation for you to present to the Maharaja. That should make things easier. It's only a little country, and he won't want to offend the British. We're a growing force in this part of the world, you know. Of course, the French would like to be top dog, but we shall prevail, you mark my words."

Jack was puzzled. Why would a Maharaja have to worry about the British? Surely he was in charge in his own country? And what did the French have to do with it?

But Uncle Edmund was nodding wisely. Jack would ask him to explain it all later. If he asked Colonel Kydd, he'd be in for another lecture.

"And… er, the Maharaja… will he help us to hire porters and so forth?" asked his uncle.

"Well, probably not in person. But there's a chap called Inchmore. He's the agent for the British East India Company – our man in Changkot, as it were. He's a good fellow, he'll help with all the practical stuff, don't you worry."

The next day, Jack woke to see brilliant sunlight streaming through the white muslin curtains. He jumped out of bed and bounded downstairs, and found Uncle Edmund helping himself to a dish made from rice, eggs and fish. Colonel Kydd said it was called kedgeree, and Jack thought it was very good.

CHAPTER FOUR

"When will we be able to go north to Hakkim, Uncle?" he said as he munched toast and honey and drank some sort of delicious fruit juice.

"Soon, Jack – soon. I can hardly believe it! In – what? A couple of weeks perhaps? Not long, anyway – we'll actually be in the Himalayas. Can you imagine it? You and I, on the roof of the world!"

It was settled that they would leave at the beginning of the following week. The Colonel assured them that this would be enough time to make the necessary preparations.

"I suppose you won't have time now to come and see my botanic garden?" said Colonel Kydd. He sounded wistful, and Uncle Edmund looked at him sympathetically.

"I wouldn't miss it for the world!" he declared. "It will give us a taste of the kind of plants we're hoping to see in Hakkim, Jack, won't it?"

Jack was horrified. The thought of trailing round after these two exclaiming over one boring plant after another certainly did *not* appeal. He was sure he could find something *much* more interesting to do.

"I think I might stay here," he said quickly.

Uncle Edmund looked at him over the top of his spectacles. "Why?" he asked.

"Um – well, you know, I thought it might be a good idea to start packing."

"Hm. Or, on the other hand, you might take it into your head to go exploring the streets of Calcutta, as you did the streets of London. No, I think you'd better come with us, Jack. There might not be anyone to rescue you if you got into trouble here."

How much longer could his uncle and the Colonel possibly spend wittering on about plants? Jack hung back to see if he could find anything better to do – but, just at that point, the Colonel began to talk about something that sounded a little more interesting. He moved closer to listen.

"…A blue rhododendron, you say? I have heard tales of a hidden valley, somewhere in Hakkim, where rhododendrons of every kind grow in remarkable profusion. On a holy mountain, it's said. There are supposed to be species there that grow nowhere else. If there *is* a blue rhododendron, that's the place to find it – you may count on it. The snag is that it's supposed to be impossible to enter this valley, because it has some kind of fearsome guardian. But of course, that's nonsense – just a story."

"In Hakkim, you say?" said Uncle Edmund , sounding interested. "Do you know the name of this mountain?"

Colonel Kydd shook his head. "No, I'm afraid not. Or did it?… Yes, it might have begun with a Z. Wouldn't swear to it, but it might have."

CHAPTER FOUR

"What's the guardian like?" asked Jack eagerly.

The Colonel laughed. "I don't know. Big, like a bear, I've heard. Or some say it's more like a giant ape. All anyone's ever seen is giant footprints... But I wouldn't get too excited about it, my boy. It's just make-believe. These people believe all kinds of nonsense."

But Jack wondered. It was their country, he thought. Surely they knew more about it than Colonel Kydd.

CHAPTER FIVE

North by Water

To reach Hakkim, they had to cross the northern plains of India. Uncle Edmund got out a map to show Jack.

"Look – the plains stretch all the way from where we are, here, in Calcutta, to the Himalayas up *here*. And this is the River Ganges. It's the greatest river in India – it starts up here in the north-west, look, and then all these other rivers join it as it flows across the plains all the way down towards Calcutta. It'll be quite a sight, I'm sure…"

But neither the thin blue line shown on the map nor Uncle Edmund's words did anything to prepare him for what the Ganges was actually like. He had seen the River Thames when he'd stayed with his uncle in London: even that seemed huge compared to the brooks and streams he was used to at home. But this river was so wide that at some points you couldn't even see the other side. It was massive.

To Jack's eyes, the boat they had hired was an odd-looking vessel, but he soon understood that it was perfectly designed for navigating, not just the Ganges, but also the shallow network of waterways which would take them north across the plains. It had a single square-rigged mast, but when there was no wind the sailors used oars to move the boat along. It was flat-bottomed so that it wouldn't get stuck on any of the many sand-bars, but, just in case, a man stood in the bow with a long wooden pole, poking it into the river to check that the water was deep enough. There were cabins, a sitting room and a dining room for the comfort of the passengers – but Jack longed to be out with the crew, eating and sleeping with only the sky for a roof.

The journey was slow, but he wasn't bored at all. There was so much to observe. He liked it best in the evening and early morning when the sun shone through milky ribbons of mist. Dimly seen shapes moved along the bank, and sometimes there was a soft splash as some mysterious beast slid into the river. Who could tell what might be lurking in the undergrowth? Once, Jack spotted a line of elephants, trunks swaying and great ears flapping gently, and he laughed out loud at the monkeys that swung through the trees on the bank. But the only creatures he saw close up were long, grey shapes lying almost submerged in the shallows, which his uncle said were crocodiles.

"Evil things," said his uncle, with a shudder. "Huge mouths crammed with rows of teeth. Apparently they eat people if they get half a chance. Still, we're safe so long as we're on the boat." He looked sharply at Jack. "You do understand that, don't you, Jack?"

"Of course," said Jack indignantly. "I'm not stupid!"

But one morning he woke up early. He'd heard a cry, quickly stifled; not a person, he thought, but an animal in pain. The boat was moored close to the bank. He tiptoed out of the cabin and went quietly up on deck, careful not to wake anyone; perhaps there might be animals coming down to the water to drink. He imagined he was by himself, on his own expedition. Or better still, that Will was with him, and they were about to set off exploring.

Then he tensed up. The tall reeds were rippling, though there was no wind. Something was moving through them, he realized – something big and powerful. What could it be?

It took only a second to swing himself over the side and drop lightly onto the bank.

He caught a glimpse of a glossy bronze coat, a ripple of powerful muscle. For a second, he hesitated, remembering what his uncle had said. But it was too good a chance to miss – he would lose track of the creature if he didn't hurry. It would be all right, he told himself. He'd be back before Uncle Edmund even knew he was gone. He plunged into the reeds.

The undergrowth thinned and came to an end. He was on the edge of a clearing, surrounded by trees. On the opposite side, lying down under a tree, was the most amazing animal he'd ever seen. Its sleek copper coat was patterned with black stripes, and it was huge! It hadn't seen him, or if it had, it was ignoring him. It seemed to be completely absorbed in washing itself, like an enormous cat, licking its paws to get to the places that were difficult to reach, like behind its ears. A tiger!

Jack almost forgot to breathe. He could hardly believe he had managed to get this close.

The tiger raised its massive head. Its green eyes gleamed. It gazed calmly at Jack, and he stood very still, entranced.

Then a shout somewhere behind him shattered the silence. The tiger rose, its powerful shoulder muscles rippling. Every movement was so smooth, so graceful. It was in its element: it was Jack who was the intruder. Turning away, it glided into the darkness between the trees.

Suddenly the glade was full. Everyone was there, his uncle, the boatmen, other passengers. The boatmen carried sticks and long, fierce-looking knives; they were all talking at once.

"Jack, are you all right? We saw tracks – they said it was a tiger!" gasped Uncle Edmund. Jack opened his mouth to try to explain to his uncle the immensity of what he had seen, but then he looked at the knives. He'd always fancied himself as a hunter, a trapper; but he found he couldn't bear the thought of anyone hunting down the tiger.

"Oh no," he said quickly. "I saw something, and so I followed it, but it was just some kind of a deer, that's all."

"Oh, thank goodness! But Jack, have you no sense at all? This is a dangerous place – how many times must I tell you that you're not in Little Stinchcombe now? You could have been killed! This simply won't do. How am I ever going to be able to trust you? Just when I start to think you've learnt some sense…"

Jack didn't bother to listen. He wasn't sorry at all. Seeing the tiger had been one of the very best moments of his life – ever.

CHAPTER SIX

Changkot

As they left the plains behind and the ground began to rise, the air grew fresher. Jack was excited. These might only be foothills, but they were higher by far than any English hills he'd seen. Soon they would reach Changkot, and not long after that they'd be in the Himalayas themselves – the highest mountains in the whole world. He couldn't wait!

The first person they met in Changkot was Mr Inchmore, the British Resident. Jack liked him immediately. He was tall and wiry, with a spring in his step that seemed as if it would bounce him easily to the other side of the Himalayas and back again. Jack was fascinated by his bushy eyebrows. He could move them completely independently of each other; they wriggled about on his face like energetic caterpillars.

"Delighted to meet you!" he cried, bounding out from his house to greet them. "Can't tell you what a pleasure it is to have guests! And you want to go off and hunt for *plants*? Extraordinary thing! I'm a butterfly man myself. Fantastic specimens hereabouts – you wouldn't believe the size of them, or the colours. Simply marvellous. Come along, come along – you must be dying of thirst. Anjuli will bring us sherbet. Have you had any yet? It's the most delicious drink you'll ever taste, I promise you. Don't worry about your baggage, Dorje will sort all that out."

"Oh – thank you," said Uncle Edmund, looking a little anxious. "But I had better keep an eye on my scientific instruments – they're very precious – you will understand, I'm sure…"

A little later, over frosted glasses of pale lemon sherbet, Uncle Edmund showed Mr Inchmore the letter of recommendation which Colonel Kydd had obtained for him.

"The Colonel said that I must present this to the Maharaja," he said. Mr Inchmore nodded.

"Yes, that should help."

"Help?" said Uncle Edmund, sounding a little anxious. "There's not likely to be any problem, is there? Nothing that could stop our expedition from proceeding?"

Mr Inchmore wrinkled his nose, and one eyebrow shot up and then down. "I trust not," he said. "But things are a little unsettled at the moment. I can't put my finger on it, but something's not quite right. Something, or someone, is afoot... Still, I can't see why anyone should object to you charging off and collecting a few plants. No, I'm sure it'll all be fine."

But unfortunately, Mr Inchmore was wrong. A court official brought the Maharaja's reply to them a few days later, and it was not the answer they were expecting. The Maharaja, the official informed them politely, was most definitely *not* minded to allow Mr Edmund Pascoe and Master Jack Fortune to travel freely within his kingdom, despite the fact that His Majesty King George III had *requested*, not to mention *required*, him to allow them to do so.

The answer, in short, was a very firm "No".

Uncle Edmund stared at the official in bewilderment. "But why?" he said. "I don't understand!"

The official bowed politely. "His Highness regrets, but the fact unfortunately is that no foreigner may travel freely in the sacred kingdom of Hakkim. He is sorry that you were not previously informed of this. Your expedition may not take place. I am sorry." He bowed again and left.

Jack was stunned. Was that it – the end of all their dreams? And then he looked at his uncle, and perceived that it was much, much worse for him.

"Uncle?" said Jack anxiously.

His uncle sank down onto a chair, as if his legs would no longer hold him up. He looked shattered. "How can this be?" he said in bewilderment. "Are they saying that we've travelled thousands of miles, come halfway round the world – for *nothing*?"

Clearly, his uncle was so utterly crushed that he was incapable of any action.

But there must be a way to save the expedition! Uncle Edmund might be prepared to give up and go home, but he certainly wasn't. Didn't his uncle realize that "No" hardly ever meant "No"? It just meant you had to find another angle of attack. So for instance, when Aunt Constance had taken it into her head that it wasn't fitting for him to play with Will Puddy because he was "just the black-smith's boy", Jack hadn't wasted time arguing. He'd simply put it to Mr Prout that it would be better if, instead of having lessons in the afternoon, he did some healthy outdoors activity instead. That way Mr Prout had a little snooze, Jack played with Will and Aunt Constance was none the wiser. Perfect. If something couldn't be shifted, you just had to find a way round it.

Not that he was thinking they could sneak into Hakkim behind the Maharaja's back. He knew that wouldn't work. No. He needed advice from locals. He needed Mr Inchmore.

When Jack began to tell him about the Maharaja's decision, Mr Inchmore had just one eyebrow lowered, so that he looked simply quizzical. By the time he'd finished, the other one had shot down to join it, creating a spectacular scowl.

"Hm," he mused. "My guess is that it's something to do with the divan."

Jack stared at him. A divan? Wasn't that some kind of sofa?

"Mr Inchmore," he said firmly, "we really have to do something. I don't know about any divans, but my uncle—"

"Call me George," said Mr Inchmore. "There aren't lots of divans, thank goodness, there's just the one. That's quite enough. You spell it D-E-W-A-N. He's the Maharaja's chief minister. He's no friend to the British, but it's not just that, there's something else going on, I'm convinced of it. There's something positively shifty about the Dewan – I wouldn't trust him an inch. The Maharaja himself is a splendid fellow – cares a great deal about his country, as you'd expect – but I can't see why he'd have a problem with you and your uncle going off and bagging a few plants."

He sat and pondered for a minute, and then he sprang up. "Come on. We'll get your uncle, and we'll go and see him."

"Who – the Maharaja? Now?"

"Why not? It's either a misunderstanding, or it's something to do with the Dewan, and either way, we're going to sort it out. Right?"

"Right!" said Jack happily. Everything was going to be resolved and, on top of that, he was going to meet a Maharaja – why, it was practically the same as going to see King George! Oh, he was going to have *so* much to tell Will about when he saw him again...

Soon, Jack, Mr Inchmore and Uncle Edmund were climbing through steep, narrow streets on their way to the palace. Jack looked round avidly. It wasn't at all like Calcutta. Not that he'd really seen that much of Calcutta, what with it being the tail end of the monsoon and not being allowed out by himself, so it wasn't really fair to judge, but he felt certain he liked Changkot *much* better. The buildings were tall and painted in bright colours, with quaint curving roofs shaped like broad-brimmed hats. The people were bright too – scarlet tunics, blue sashes, turquoise earrings, white teeth and brown skin. He stared at them inquisitively, and they stared right back and grinned at him. They seemed very friendly. He didn't see why they were laughing so much, though. He began to wonder if he'd got something on his face, and wiped it surreptitiously.

"Don't worry," advised Mr Inchmore. "They just think you look funny because you're different, you see. Everyone comes here," he went on, looking round with pleasure. "There are lots of different tribes who live in the mountains, and Changkot's the place where all of them come and trade. So much to look at, isn't there?"

Then, between two houses, Jack saw something that stopped him in his tracks. In the distance he could make out immense mountains with snow glistening on their peaks. "Look, Uncle!" he breathed.

His uncle stood still. He didn't say a word, and Jack glanced at him. He was gazing at the faraway peaks with a look of the most desperate longing on his face. Jack suddenly saw just how much his uncle wanted – no, needed – to reach them. On impulse, he touched his arm and said seriously, "It'll be all right, Uncle Edmund. We *will* get there. I promise you we will."

His uncle looked surprised. Then he smiled sadly. "I hope so, Jack," he said. "Oh, I do hope so!"

Mr Inchmore led them on. The palace sat high up above the town, surrounded by trees and gardens. For once, Uncle Edmund didn't dart about identifying flowers. He was tense and pale. But Jack gazed round with great interest. He'd never been to a palace before, and didn't think he was likely to again, so he was determined to take it all in.

The doorways and windows were framed with carved wooden panels and columns, picked out in red, turquoise and gold leaf. The roof rose in tiers, each smaller than the last, and each decorated with snarling gilded dragons with scarlet tongues and emerald eyes. Jack loved it, and thought King George's palace probably wasn't half as nice.

Mr Inchmore bowed deeply, and asked the official who came to greet them to present his compliments to the Maharaja, and to beg an audience for himself and his visitors, who had travelled far across the ocean to meet him. It seemed hours before the official came back, but eventually he did. Jack breathed a deep sigh of relief when he indicated that they were to follow him up flights of white marble stairs, which eventually led to a room at the very top of a high tower.

Jack decided it was the best room he'd ever seen. There were windows everywhere, and they were wide open to the sky. It was like the best tree house you could possibly imagine, he thought. Or not a tree house – a sky house. And there, in the distance, unobstructed by any other buildings, was another view of those beautiful mountains.

Jack had thought that the Maharaja would be sitting on a throne. But he wasn't. He was sitting on the floor among a pile of blue and crimson silk cushions. His legs were crossed, and though he looked quite old to Jack, his back was straight.

Jack had never seen a maharaja, and he hadn't really known what to expect. But there had been a portrait in Colonel Kydd's house of an Indian emperor. He'd worn a turban decorated with enormous jewels and peacock feathers, and had ropes of pearls and rubies round his neck. Jack had imagined that the Maharaja would look something like this.

But he didn't. The Indian emperor's face had been soft and plump, but this man had a face that could have been carved out of oak, smooth and gleaming. He had sharply angled cheekbones and his eyes were dark and lively. He wore a small embroidered cap, not a turban, and a simple brown robe with an orange sash.

The Maharaja's gaze was direct and alert, and Jack liked him immediately. He knew straight away that here was one adult he would never play a trick on or lie to. The only other person he'd felt like that about was Will Puddy's father, the blacksmith, who had a very strong right arm – and a left one too, for that matter. You wouldn't want to be on the wrong side of an argument with Mr Puddy, and you wouldn't want the Maharaja to think badly of you. Jack bowed very deeply to him, without having to be told, and Mr Inchmore began to speak. Jack was impressed that he seemed to be fluent in the Hakkim language.

The Maharaja smiled courteously and gestured that they should join him on the floor among the cushions. Servants offered them apricots and almonds from small bowls, and sherbet in tiny green translucent cups. Uncle Edmund held his cup up to the light.

"Why, surely this is jade," he said, admiring it.

"Indeed," said the Maharaja. "It is beautiful, is it not? Like light shining through water."

Uncle Edmund looked at him in surprise, and the Maharaja's face creased in merriment. "You did not expect that I would speak your language? Ah – we are far from Calcutta here, but in India these days one is never far from the British. Your people are everywhere! To get to know your friend, as well as your enemy, it is necessary to understand his language. So I have employed tutors to teach me English, and also to teach it to my children." He leant back and gazed at Jack and his uncle. "And which, I wonder, are you? Friends, or enemies?"

He wasn't smiling any longer, and Jack stared at him, dismayed. Why should he think they might be enemies? Mr Inchmore began to speak.

"Your Highness, please let me assure you that—"

Suddenly, Jack heard an angry voice and a clash of metal outside the room. Startled, he turned to see the massive figure of a man in the doorway. The guards had barred his way with crossed swords, but the Maharaja nodded to them, and they stood aside to let him through.

He bowed deeply to the Maharaja, his hands together as if he was praying – but the glance he directed at Uncle Edmund, Mr Inchmore and Jack was pure poison. Jack glared back. Who did he think he was, looking at them like that? He was very richly dressed, much more so than the Maharaja. Beneath a white turban decorated with a jewelled clasp, his eyes were dark and hooded, and the lower half of his face was almost hidden by a thick, bushy beard. He wore a closely fitting tunic fastened with a row of small buttons made of pearls set in gold, and round his neck hung chains and ropes of jewels. He spoke quickly to the Maharaja, waving his arm contemptuously in the direction of poor Uncle Edmund, who looked completely bewildered.

"The Dewan," muttered Mr Inchmore. "Frightful bounder."

The Maharaja turned to them. "Please excuse the manner of my chief minister's arrival. He is inspired by his desire to safeguard Hakkim from the grasp of foreigners. He reminds me that where one European enters" – at this point, the Dewan shot a venomous look towards Mr Inchmore – "many others inevitably follow, as they have elsewhere in India. They do not always respect our ways – they do not always respect *us*. This is a remote kingdom but, nevertheless, news comes to us of what is happening in the south. We know that in some parts of India the British rule in all but name.

Your East India Company is powerful, and it grows ever stronger. When a tiger hunts, it seeks out the weakest first. I think that the Company is like this too. Hakkim is small and less wealthy than some other states – but we are not weak, and we will not be swallowed.

"This being said, I do not know if we should fear you, Mr Pascoe. You do not seem to be of a kind with most of the other members of the Company I have met. And yet the crocodile lies like a log for much of his life – but when he finally wakes, he is as danger-ous as any tiger. Mr Inchmore asks me to change my mind and allow you to travel freely in my country. So, Mr Pascoe, tell me why I should do this? What do you want from Hakkim?"

For a moment, Uncle Edmund was quiet, choosing his words. Jack very much hoped they would be the right ones. Otherwise their expedition would be over before it had even begun.

At last, Uncle Edmund began to speak. "I am a natu-ralist – a botanist, to be exact. My interest – I might almost say my passion – is in plants. To a botanist, your country is remarkable for the variety of its habitats. Within a small area, it has both tropical forests and alpine meadows. I have never before seen either. I ask only for the privilege – and believe me, I know very well what a tremendous privilege it is – of recording the extraordi-nary variety of plants which, to the best of my belief, grow in the valleys and on the mountains of Hakkim. If Your Highness permits, I will also gather seed. This I will take back to England. King George has established a great botanical garden at Kew, near London, where he hopes to gather plants from all over the world. Nothing would give me greater pleasure than to present him with plants grown from seed gathered here. In this way, the people of Britain would be fortunate enough to share in the beauty of the plants of Hakkim.

"Truly, Your Highness, this is all I ask. I assure you that if you allow me to travel in Hakkim, I will tread lightly on your land. I will take nothing from it that it cannot easily spare."

Jack felt like clapping. He'd had no idea his uncle could be so eloquent. The Dewan was scowling and obviously wanted to say something, but the Maharaja held up his hand to tell him to wait.

"Plants? That is all you want from us – just plants? But – you say you want to record them. How will you do that, Mr Pascoe? Can you explain to me?"

It suddenly struck Jack that here was something he could help with. As usual, he had his father's bag slung over his shoulder. He shrugged it off, knelt down and began to rummage through it. In an instant, the guards moved forward, their hands on the hilts of their swords, their expressions fierce. Jack stared in surprise, then suddenly understood they must think he was about to pull out a weapon. Aware that Uncle Edmund and Mr Inchmore were both looking anxious, he hastily brandished his father's sketchbook. The guards retreated, with one last scowl for luck.

Jack wasn't quite sure how he should address the Maharaja, but he thought it was a pretty safe bet that plenty of bowing would be in order, so he did a very deep one for starters and then held the book out towards him. He thought he'd better not get too close, in case the guards got excited again. Really, he thought, everyone was so touchy!

"This is how we record plants, Your Highness, sir," he explained. "We draw them."

The Maharaja leant forward. "Really? May I see? Come – show them to me."

Uncle Edmund looked at Jack in surprise, and Jack realized he'd never shown any of his drawings to him. In fact, the last time they'd spoken about drawing, months ago back in London, he'd said he had no interest in drawing. He smiled at his uncle apologetically, and then settled himself on the cushion the Maharaja had patted and leafed through the book till he came to the drawings he had done in the garden in London. The Maharaja turned the pages slowly. Mr Inchmore and Uncle Edmund watched with interest, and the Dewan seethed and glowered in the background.

"I see, I see… And it is you who has drawn these pictures? This one too?"

He was pointing at the picture of Jack's mother.

"No, Your Highness. I didn't do that one – my father did. It's my mother."

"Your father? You mean Mr Pascoe? But no – I think Mr Inchmore gave you a different name. You are called—"

"Fortune, sir. Jack Fortune. Mr Pascoe is my uncle."

He looked puzzled. "And your parents are happy that you travel so far from them?"

Jack sighed. He hated talking about his parents – he didn't want people feeling sorry for him. "My parents are dead, sir. They died when I was little. I never knew them. My father was an artist, and he painted these pictures in Venice. He liked travelling, you see. I like it too. And so does Uncle Edmund. Well, he does now," he added, remembering that up till now his uncle had never left England.

The Maharaja turned back to the pictures Jack had done, and studied them. "And so you are an artist, like your father."

"Oh no, sir," said Jack hastily. "I'm going to be an explorer, not an artist. I just draw a little bit. Sometimes. I just wanted to show you how the plants can be recorded, sir."

The Maharaja looked at Uncle Edmund. "I see," he said. "Well, I am sure you will be most useful to your uncle, Jack Fortune." He fell silent, deep in thought. The moments turned into minutes. Jack sat as still as he could, hoping against hope that, between them, they'd said enough to persuade him.

At last, he looked at them. "My oldest son is called Thondup. Like you, he is curious to learn more of the world. He will accompany you – he will enjoy it, and he can translate for you. Also, he will tell you if there are places where you may not go. For there are such places – sacred places, which are forbidden to strangers. If you agree to this, then I will give you my blessing." He looked at the Dewan, who clearly understood what had been said and didn't like it one little bit, and nodded calmly. "It shall be so. The Dewan will find a guide for you and give you what further assistance is necessary."

The Dewan drew himself up very tall. His eyes flashed angrily, and he looked as if he'd like to hit either Jack or his uncle or Mr Inchmore – or, better still, all three of them. He bowed to the Maharaja, then whirled round. Jack wouldn't have been at all surprised if he'd disappeared in a puff of smoke, like any other evil genie, but disappointingly he just went through the door the same as anyone else.

Mr Inchmore's eyebrows were doing overtime as he watched this spectacular performance, but Uncle Edmund was so delighted he hardly noticed. The Maharaja turned and gave them a dazzling smile.

CHAPTER SIX

"Forgive the Dewan. He is discourteous, but it is only because he cares so deeply about Hakkim. Jack Fortune, there is one more thing. When you return, I would like you to come and see me. Will you do that? Will you come and tell me about your journey?"

Jack bowed so deeply he almost fell over, and promised solemnly that he would. This Thondup was lucky, Jack decided, having a father like the Maharaja.

Outside the palace, they were all so excited they just couldn't stay still. Mr Inchmore and Jack did a bouncy little victory dance, and Uncle Edmund grinned and hopped awkwardly from one foot to another. Then they went through the whole interview again: "Wasn't it funny when…" and "Did you see the look on the Dewan's face when…" and "You really saved the day when…" and all that kind of thing.

Finally, Uncle Edmund cleared his throat and said solemnly: "I just want to say, Jack, that I know I have you to thank for this. I was ready to give up for a moment there, I must admit. The success of this expedition means more to me than you know, but if it hadn't been for you and our friend Mr Inchmore here, we'd be packing to go home at this very moment. All I can say is – well, my sister Constance's loss is very much my gain. I feel privileged to have you with me, Jack."

It was an unusual experience for Jack to have a grown-up saying nice things to him. He blushed and cleared his throat, and looked anywhere but at his uncle, and then in the nick of time Mr Inchmore stepped in and changed the subject.

"Well," he said, "that's all very fine. But we mustn't waste any time, you know – there's an expedition to be organized. Where you're going the paths are narrow and steep – too treacherous for horses. You'll need a team of porters to carry everything – food as well as all your equipment. Though you should be able to barter for fresh food on the way. I wish I could come with you," he said wistfully.

"Oh – couldn't you?" said Jack eagerly.

Mr Inchmore shook his head regretfully. "I need to keep an eye on things here. I really don't feel happy about the Dewan. I didn't trust him before, but after today's performance – well! All that about caring deeply for Hakkim – I don't know, it doesn't ring true to me. I suspect he only cares deeply about himself. He doesn't even come from this country originally – nobody quite seems to know where he's from. Anyway, he's certainly got it in for the British, and it's my job to make sure our interests are protected. But keep an eye out for butterflies, won't you, young Jack? Perhaps you might even manage to sketch some for me."

Jack promised he would. It was, he thought, the very least he could do.

CHAPTER SEVEN

Into the Jungle

It was the evening before their departure. They were
to leave just after dawn, while it was still cool. The
first part of their journey would take them through
jungle, and Mr Inchmore warned them that the heat
would be almost unbearable. He looked approvingly
at the new, lightweight clothes they'd had made in
Calcutta.

"Make sure you don't leave any skin uncovered on
your legs," he warned.

Uncle Edmund nodded wisely. "Snakes, you mean."

"Hm? Yes, snakes are a danger, it's true. They hang
from the trees, you know. Look just like creepers – till
they attack. Yes, you should certainly watch out for
them. But I was actually thinking of leeches."

"Leeches?" said Jack, puzzled. "They're those things Dr Jennings uses, aren't they? Once Aunt Constance was ill, and he brought some in a jar. Black, they were, and slimy. He said they were going to suck her blood." He smiled happily, remembering.

"Mm," said Mr Inchmore. "That's right. Useful little chappies. This is where they come from. Well, one of the places. First time I went out in the jungle, I looked down after a few hours, and there they were, all latched on to my legs above my socks. Bit of a shock, I don't mind telling you. All glistening and fat and heaving. With my blood."

Jack gulped, imagining what it would feel like to have all the blood sucked out of his legs. He'd collapse, most likely. He determined to tuck his trousers firmly into his socks, no matter how hot it was.

"Well, thank you for that," said Uncle Edmund faintly. "We'll certainly look out for them. Er... come along, Jack. I'll show you our route on the map."

He spread the map out on the table, and pointed out Changkot.

"We go south-west from here, along this valley, till we reach the River Dalpo. Then, as far as possible, we'll follow its course north, until we reach the mountains. That way, part of the journey will be in the jungle, and part in the mountains. Two very different habitats, Jack. Most interesting."

"I see," said Jack, determined to stay concentrated. "And we pull lots of plants up as we go."

"Er… well, something like that. We don't exactly pull them up. And as I told the Maharaja, we have to record all sorts of information about them too. Everything in nature is connected, you see, Jack. Different plants grow in different kinds of terrain—"

"Terrain? What's that?"

"A terrain is a particular kind of landscape," explained Uncle Edmund. "If you want to get plants to grow, you need to know what sorts of rock they grow on, what kind of weather they like, the sort of insects that like them – all kinds of things."

"So you have to collect them, and draw them, and write about them?" Jack thought about this. It sounded like a lot of work. "But why?"

Uncle Edmund looked puzzled. "Why?"

"Yes, why? Why are we doing it? What's the point?"

Uncle Edmund spluttered. "What's the *point*? Weren't you listening when I explained it to the Maharaja just the other day? Oh, all right. Let me see if I can get you to understand. The first thing quite simply is that, if you're a scientist, you want to know how things work. I'm a botanist, so I want to know about plants. I want to know why a blue gentian will only grow on a mountain, and an orchid will only grow in a jungle."

Jack thought about this. He wasn't convinced that it entirely explained why his uncle had suddenly decided to up sticks and travel halfway round the world.

"So that's the first thing," he said. "What's the second?"

Uncle Edmund ran his hand through his hair. "The second? Ah, well now, let me see. Plants are useful for food. Think of tea and coffee, for instance. Only a few years ago we'd never heard of them in Britain, and now we couldn't do without them. We might find something like that – something that would make our fortune."

Jack perked up. This sounded much more interesting.

"And another thing," Uncle Edmund went on. "People will pay a lot of money to have something new and exotic for their gardens."

"Will they?" said Jack doubtfully.

"Oh yes! Not ordinary people, but lords and dukes and… and… people like that. And then, when they see how desirable a plant is, the ordinary people will want it too."

"So that's what we're looking for? Something new?"

"Yes. And I have a particular plant in mind," said Uncle Edmund, his cheeks pink with enthusiasm. "You remember the rhododendrons Colonel Kydd showed us in his botanic garden?"

Jack frowned. The botanic garden was a bit of a blur.

"Big trees?" said Uncle Edmund, waving his pipe about to demonstrate. "Glossy dark green leaves? Lots of flower buds?"

Jack's face cleared. Colonel Kydd had told that very interesting story about a hidden valley and a powerful guardian.

"Yes? Well, they come in lots of different colours. But no one's ever found a blue one. As I said to the Colonel, I'm convinced there must be one, and if I could find it, it would make my name, Jack! I'd be famous! Imagine it – *Rhododendron pascoensis*!"

His eyes were shining, he'd run his fingers through his hair so it was standing on end and he looked at least ten years younger than the timid, rather nervous Uncle Edmund who'd turned up at Coombe Lodge all those months ago. Jack suddenly felt very fond of him. After all, he could have chosen to leave Jack in a school or with a tutor, despite what Jack's mother had said, but he hadn't. Jack would make sure he didn't regret it, he decided, feeling very noble and quite misty-eyed. From now on, he was going to be absolutely sensible and completely reliable. Aunt Constance had thought he was an idiot. Well, he wasn't. And he was going to prove it.

By noon the next day, he wasn't feeling quite so keen. It already felt as if they'd been trudging through the jungle for ever. At the head of the procession was Sonam, their guide. Jack approved of Sonam. He looked like a proper explorer. His skin was like dark-brown leather, burnt by the sun and wind, and there were creases at the outer corners of his eyes, which Jack thought were probably the result of long days peering into the distance. He wore a large piece of bright turquoise in one earlobe, which gave him an interestingly raffish look. A knife hung in a sheath from his belt.

Behind him were Jack and the Maharaja's son Thondup, who was older than Jack – almost a grown-up. Apparently being the Maharaja's son made him a prince. Jack wasn't sure what to make of him yet. He couldn't help but wonder if someone used to living in a palace was really going to be much use on an expedition like this.

Then there was a long procession of porters, each carrying a huge pack. Jack couldn't keep track of his uncle; ever since they'd entered the jungle, Uncle Edmund had been leaping about all over the place, capering from one tree or flower to the next with cries of enthusiasm. Jack didn't know where he got the energy.

He wiped the sweat off his forehead and wondered how long it would be before they stopped for lunch. He didn't like this heat. It wasn't a *nice* kind of heat. It made his skin prickle. The worst of it was that he had to keep every inch of himself covered because of the leeches, and his clothes clung unpleasantly – but he'd rather be hot and sticky than have all his blood sucked out – he was quite clear about that.

There was so much water about. If it wasn't actually raining, water dripped from the trees anyway, so it still felt as if it was. He looked up at the canopy of branches above, but they were almost hidden by mist – or was it low cloud? It was very difficult to tell. He brushed a creeper away from his face. The forest was full of tendrils, twisting and twining round anything that wasn't actually moving – when Jack complained about them, his uncle had said that all the trees and plants were trying to scramble up out of the dense, dark shade of the rainforest and towards the sun.

"They're just like us," he said cheerfully, "they want to reach the light."

Thondup stopped, so suddenly that Jack barged into him.

"Look!" said the prince, pointing.

There was a gap between the trees. The clouds had drifted apart, and suddenly there it was – a great mountain with towering peaks and pinnacles, like a silver castle floating in the sky. Jack stood and stared.

"It takes your breath away," he said softly.

The prince glanced at him, a little surprised. "Indeed it does! It is Zemu, the sacred mountain."

"Sacred?" asked Jack, puzzled. "What do you mean? How can a mountain be sacred?" *Sacred* had to do with church and the Bible, Mr Prout's boring sermons – that kind of thing – not mountains.

Then he remembered that just outside Changkot they'd passed a monastery. It had been a jolly-looking place, painted in bright colours and surrounded by triangular flags fluttering from poles stuck into the ground. The prince had explained that the flags had prayers written on them, and the wind took these messages and whispered them throughout the world, so that they might touch and soften the hearts of all they met. Jack had been very taken with this idea, and he'd entertained the idea of sending a message to Aunt Constance. It could say something like "Having a wonderful time, glad you're not here".

"Is there a monastery on the mountain?" he asked Prince Thondup. "Is that why it's sacred?"

The prince smiled. "There is indeed a monastery. It is at the foot of the mountain. But it is there because the mountain is holy – not the other way around. No: the mountain is sacred because the god himself sits up there, high among the glaciers and peaks, surrounded by ice and snow."

Jack looked at him doubtfully. Mr Prout had definitely given the impression that God lived in heaven, floating on fluffy clouds and surrounded by angels. "Are you sure?" he said.

Prince Thondup nodded, his eyes merry. He seemed to think it was quite funny that Jack was so ignorant. "Oh yes," he said, "Mount Zemu is the god's home. From there he controls the rain and the snow. We must treat him with respect, or he will send down terrible floods, or... what do you call them? When snow and stones move, and roar down the mountain like an angry lion?" He made dramatic swooshing movements to demonstrate, and Jack ducked hastily.

"Um... avalanches?" he suggested.

"Yes, even so, those. In the autumn, to honour him, there is a great festival. People go there from all over the country, and the priests dress in colourful costumes and dance. But it is forbidden for any save the priests to go beyond the monastery. Mount Zemu is the holiest place in all Hakkim."

As they gazed respectfully at the mountain, Uncle Edmund caught them up, clutching a curving stem of white flowers. He beamed. "It's an orchid – a type of *Cypripedium*, I believe. Isn't it exquisite? We must certainly try to get some specimens safely back to England, though I fear it will prove difficult... But what were you looking at?"

Jack pointed towards the gap in the trees and said, "That's Mount Zemu. Prince Thondup's been telling me all about it."

"Has he?"

"Yes. It's a holy mountain. It's got a god living on it, so no one's allowed to go there."

"Really? Now what does that remind me of?..." He gazed at the mountain in its frame of trees. "What an extraordinary sight! The roof of the world, Jack, the roof of the world! Can you believe that it's so close?"

As they watched, the clouds swirled in front of the mountain and it disappeared from view. Uncle Edmund sighed with satisfaction. "A thrilling sight. We have been privileged. Now – I think we might look for a place to camp soon, er... Your Highness..."

The prince bowed courteously. "Please, Mr Pascoe and Jack Fortune, call me Thondup. It is not necessary to use my title."

"And you can just call me Jack," said Jack generously.

"Thank you, Your Highness... er, Thondup," said Uncle Edmund, bowing back. "Most kind. We are honoured. Well, as I was saying, it's rather early I know, but this area is extremely rich in epiphytal orchids – those are orchids that actually grow on trees, Jack, rather than on the ground. Really remarkable. It will take me some time to collect and store as many specimens as I would like."

Jack followed Thondup, determined to help Sonam and impress him with his practical abilities. So far, the guide hadn't been very friendly, but Jack was sure that once he'd shown Sonam how useful he was, that would change.

The guide showed him how to cut lengths of wood from the jungle and tie them together to make crosspieces and a ridge pole. Jack soon got the idea, and then watched carefully as the men collected spiky leaves called bamboo and wove them round the framework to make roofs. He and Uncle Edmund had folding camp beds, and he set them up, with a table in between made of a log which Sonam had split. Uncle Edmund was full of admiration.

"Why, Jack, you've done a splendid job! Now – there's something else you could help me with, if you would."

Jack waited expectantly.

"I saw your drawings, Jack – the ones you showed to the Maharaja. It seems that you have inherited your father's talent after all."

Jack frowned. He could see where this was going, and he didn't like it.

"It would be very helpful to me if you could help with recording the plants we find. Very helpful indeed." Uncle Edmund paused expectantly.

Jack shook his head. "Oh, I don't think so," he said firmly. "I'm really not all that good. I'd be too slow, I'm sure I would. No use at all. And anyway, I'm far too busy. I've got to go and see if Sonam needs more help now – excuse me, Uncle."

He marched off. Sonam smiled when he offered to help, and Jack felt pleased. He didn't want to be like his father, and he didn't want to be an artist. He wanted to be a practical man – like Sonam. Someone who could do things. Someone sensible. Someone you could rely on.

"Come along, Jack," said his uncle, much too loudly. "It's time to get up. We must make a start before it gets too hot."

Jack groaned. Surely it couldn't be morning already?

He'd found it very difficult to get to sleep the night before. There had been all manner of strange rustlings and whisperings in the forest, and he was just a little bit concerned about the snakes which Mr Inchmore had dismissed so airily. And as if that wasn't enough, there were the insects, which all seemed to be enormous. They were attracted by his uncle's candle, and they buzzed and crawled and bit and stung. He'd tried pulling his sheet over his head, but he'd soon got far too hot.

He sat up, rubbing his eyes and yawning.

"There's a bowl of water over there," said his uncle briskly. "Have a good wash before breakfast."

"Oh, you don't bother about things like washing when you're an explorer, Uncle," explained Jack.

"But I'm not an explorer," his uncle objected, "I'm a plant hunter."

"You might not be an explorer," Jack pointed out, "but I am."

Uncle Edmund smiled. "Oh, of course. I was forgetting. So – do explorers eat breakfast?"

"Certainly," said Jack.

Come to think of it, he was feeling exceptionally hungry. Breakfast was one of his favourite meals. At Aunt Constance's he usually had it by himself, in what used to be the nursery, and it had consisted of porridge and toast. But once he'd managed to sneak out and camp overnight in the woods with Will, and Will's mum had given them thick slices of ham and eggs, very carefully wrapped so they wouldn't break, and Will had found mushrooms. They'd made a fire and fried it all up, and it had been well worth the trouble he'd got into when he got home. It had been fantastic.

What a pity Will wasn't with him now! He missed Will so much. He missed Sarah too. He even… no, no, what was he thinking? Of course he didn't miss Aunt Constance! He put the nonsensical thought out of his head and set off in search of food.

Sayan, the cook, had prepared rice balls for breakfast, with something delicious which was a sort of cross between pancake and bread, and slices of mango. Jack loved mangoes. He thought they were much nicer than apples or pears. An idea struck him.

"What do mangoes grow on?" he asked Thondup.

"Trees," said the prince.

"We should take some back to England," he said, turning to his uncle. "Everyone would love it! You could grow lots of trees and sell one to every family, and they'd be really pleased. And you'd be very rich," he added.

Uncle Edmund smiled. "Mangoes need the warmth of the Indian sun, Jack. I don't think they'd be happy with English winters. And it wouldn't be hot enough in the summer to ripen the fruits."

"Oh," said Jack, disappointed. He took another slice. "In that case, I'll just eat as much as I can while I'm here."

He wasn't so sure about the tea, though. It was called *chai*, Sayan told him.

"It is made in a special way in the mountains," explained Thondup. "We use yak butter. It is very refreshing."

"Butter? In *tea*?" said Jack. He stared at it, mesmerized. Globules of fat floated on the surface. It didn't look like any tea Jack had ever seen before.

"The yak – it's a kind of ox, isn't it?" said Uncle Edmund.

"Ah, the yak!" said Thondup. "It is a truly marvellous beast. Its hair can be woven into blankets. It provides milk, butter and cheese, and occasionally meat. It is strong, and can carry heavy weights. And without the yak, we would have no chai."

"That *would* be a shame," said Jack.

His uncle sipped his chai politely. Jack discreetly tipped his away.

For the next few days, they kept to a similar pattern, making an early start so they could trek through the jungle before the heat became unbearable, then stopping to "botanize", as Uncle Edmund called it. Jack's favourite job was climbing trees to collect leaves and flowers, though Uncle Edmund was still trying hard to interest him in the notes and drawings that had to be done.

"We must always record where a plant is found, Jack, and for this we use a compass. The thermometer is to measure the temperature, and then I have this small barometer, which will tell me how much moisture was in the air in the particular place a plant is found. If this orchid, for instance, is to grow in England, we need to know what conditions it prefers."

"But it's like you said about the mangoes, Uncle," said Jack. "*They* won't grow in England because the weather's different. So surely none of these plants will either."

Uncle Edmund looked pleased. "Do you know, I think you're beginning to get the hang of it! That's a very sensible question! You're right – they wouldn't grow if we just planted them out in Aunt Constance's back garden. But at Kew, and in the gardens of some of the great houses, like Chatsworth and Blenheim, there are vast structures made entirely of glass. They are heated, and so they can mimic the conditions we find in warmer parts of the world. So *some* people would be able to grow them, even though most people wouldn't. Now – I must do some sketches. I suppose you wouldn't…"

Jack shook his head firmly. "Sorry, Uncle, too much to do."

CHAPTER EIGHT

Hitting the Heights

After three days, they came to the River Dalpo, and the landscape began to change. Soon they were climbing up a steep gorge. The river hurtled from rock to rock, flinging spray high into the air.

The air became cooler and fresher. The path, no longer able to squeeze in beside the river, began to snake away up the cliff. After a while, Jack turned to look back down the valley. Beyond the long line of porters, each carrying a bulky pack, the jungle was a dark shadow, wreathed in mist. Jack was glad to be out of the heat. Plants might like it, but he certainly didn't. He felt much better now.

At first it was easy going, but soon the path narrowed and they had to go in single file. Jack was close behind his uncle – who suddenly, just as a pile of fallen rocks made the path even narrower, bent down to peer at a tiny plant growing out of a crack in the rock.

"Exquisite!" he murmured. "A campanula, and one I've certainly never seen before. Quite delightful…"

"Could you move on, Uncle?" said Jack. "There… er… there really isn't very much room here."

"What? Oh, yes, I see – don't worry, I'll only be a second."

Uncle Edmund tugged the plant out gently, wrapped it in tissue and stowed it carefully in his haversack. Then he turned to carry on – but as he did so, he stumbled, and a shower of small stones skittered off the path and fell over the edge of the cliff. As Jack watched, they hurtled down to the river, thousands of feet below. With horrified fascination, he imagined what would happen if he, too, fell off the path. It could happen so easily. It would just take one slip, and then he'd be spinning through the air, over and over again, his arms flailing helplessly – until, finally, he'd plummet into the river. He'd probably already be dead by then, but if he wasn't, he'd either drown or be smashed into little bits by the rocks.

He swallowed, and pressed close in against the comforting solidity of the cliff face. Look up, he told himself firmly. Up is better.

It wasn't.

The rock face reared high above him. Clouds moved across the sky. But no – it wasn't the clouds – it was the cliff itself that was moving! He stared in open-mouthed horror. Had no one else noticed? It must be an avalanche. The whole mountain was swaying and, if it fell, it would carry them all with it.

"Uncle!" he finally managed to squeak, his hands clinging to the rock.

Uncle Edmund was several yards ahead by this stage. He turned.

"Yes, Jack? What is it?" he enquired. "Goodness, you've gone a funny colour – hasn't he, Thondup?"

Thondup was waiting patiently behind Jack for him to get a move on. He grinned, and said, "Forgive me – to me your skin is always a strange colour. So pale…"

Had they no sense? What were they wittering on about? Couldn't they see what was happening? He found his voice again. "Uncle – *look*! The mountain – it's moving! Thondup, can't you see?"

Puzzled, Thondup followed Jack's gaze skyward. Then his face cleared. "Ah, I understand! No, Jack – the mountain is standing still, as always. It is only the clouds that move."

Uncle Edmund spoke soothingly. "You're a little dizzy, Jack, that's all. Don't worry about it. Just edge carefully round the rocks. The path gets wider then, and you'll be fine. Don't look so upset – you just don't like heights. There's no shame in that: lots of people don't."

Was that what it was? Jack was plunged into despair. How could he be an explorer if he was afraid of heights? He'd climbed trees, and that hadn't worried him – why should mountains be any different? He gritted his teeth. He *could* do it – he had to. He edged delicately round the rock fall, step by careful step, not looking up and not looking down. The path widened, and he began to feel better.

Then things took a turn for the worse.

A few yards farther on, they found that the path had fallen away completely, and they all came to a halt. Uncle Edmund frowned.

"Ah, Thondup – would you ask Sonam what we're going to do about this? The path seems to have come to a stop, not to put too fine a point on it."

Thondup conferred with Sonam, who pointed upwards. Far above, a thin, pale line snaked round the mountain.

"The path continues, far above," explained Thondup. "Do you see?"

"But that's up there," pointed out Jack, feeling a little nervous, "and we're down here."

Sonam must have worked out what he was saying, perhaps by the look on his face. He grinned and beckoned them to come closer.

And then Jack saw the ladder.

It was attached by wooden pegs to the sides of a narrow vertical gulley. It went a very long way up. It was made of rope, with thin wooden slats for steps, and it didn't look a bit safe – not a bit. Sonam smiled proudly.

"He can't be expecting us to go up there, can he?" whispered Jack.

Sonam nodded, and said something to Thondup.

"He says it is a very good ladder," said Thondup with an encouraging smile. "Very safe. There are many such ladders in the mountains, to help us to reach the high places in a shorter time. And he says that when we have climbed the ladder we will soon come to a place where there are many beautiful flowers."

So that was all right then.

Everyone was watching Jack expectantly. Usually, he was the first to try out anything: the first to climb a tree, the first to cross a rickety bridge, the first to use boulders as stepping stones to cross a stream. His heart sank. He couldn't do it – he just couldn't!

Uncle Edmund glanced at him, and then at the ladder. "My goodness," he said, "what fun this is! I wonder what your Aunt Constance would think if she could see us now, eh, Jack?"

He adjusted his pack more firmly on his back. Once he was satisfied that it was safe, he grasped the sides of the ladder and set off.

"One step after another, that's the ticket," he said loudly. He climbed slowly and steadily upwards, till he was a small figure crawling upwards like a beetle. At last, he reached the top.

Sonam gestured to Jack. His turn. The guide's eyes twinkled in the folds of his weather-beaten skin, and he smiled encouragingly. Jack swallowed. Sonam would think he was an idiot if he dithered any longer – they all would – and he couldn't bear that. The ladder was there, and he had to climb it. There was no other way.

He took hold of it firmly and put his right foot on the first rung. But his left leg was shaking uncontrollably, and somehow he couldn't lift it from the ground. It was the same as before, when he'd suddenly realized that one false step could lead to death. Instinct shouted at him to cling on to the ground, to safety. It was a physical feeling, as if his body was too heavy to move, and he knew for certain that there was simply no way he could force himself to climb the ladder.

Everyone was waiting for him – the ladder could only bear the weight of one person at a time. He leant his head against the cool surface of the rock and wondered what on earth he was going to do.

Someone touched his shoulder. It was Thondup. He spoke quietly, so that no one else could hear.

"You are afraid, Jack."

"No!" said Jack. Then: "Yes," he whispered.

Thondup was quiet for a moment. "But you can overcome this, and you will. Do not think about the fear. Think only about your breathing. You will draw strength into your body with each breath. Believe me, it will be so. Let your mind be calm. Now, move your hands up, one after the other, and then your feet. Think about what you are doing in each moment, and let nothing else come into your mind. Do not look up, and do not look down. You can do this."

Jack fervently hoped he was right. He closed his eyes and breathed in, concentrating on the sound of the air and the feeling of his chest as it rose and fell. Slowly, he began to feel calmer. After a minute, he opened his eyes, took a very deep breath and began to climb. First a hand, then a foot. Then the other hand, and the other foot – and then the same, all over again.

He felt relieved. The ladder might have looked rickety, but the pegs were secure. All he had to do was keep going.

He must be near the top. How much farther did he have to go? Forgetting what Thondup had said, he glanced up. Uncle Edmund was kneeling down, looking over the edge of the cliff, smiling encouragingly. Jack smiled back – and then he made a *big* mistake. He bent his neck back to look farther, beyond his uncle – and once again the clouds were racing, the mountain was moving and his head was spinning wildly. He clung on to the ladder for dear life, and knew that he would never move again. It just wasn't possible.

"Jack – Jack!" It was Uncle Edmund. His voice was clear and calm. "Come on, old fellow. You're doing very well, not far to go now. Just one step at a time: first your hand – that's it – and now your foot, then your other hand – that's the way, well done. Imagine you're climbing a tree in your aunt's garden – she's coming round the corner any minute, and you need to be up out of the way, so just keep going…"

His voice was steady, and Jack let it wash over him and felt his body begin to relax, just enough to let him move, and, as if in a dream, he carried on climbing.

Then there he was, scrambling up onto the path beside Uncle Edmund. Oh, the relief! He flung his arms round his uncle and hugged him tight.

"Oh, my goodness!" murmured Uncle Edmund, patting him on the back awkwardly. "There, there. It's over now."

They sat down to wait for the others. Uncle Edmund took his glasses off and polished them carefully, and Jack gazed at his uncle with new respect. He'd always thought that he was the strong, practical one, but today it hadn't been like that. Uncle Edmund might be a bit of a bumbler, but when it came to it, he'd come through and Jack almost hadn't. This was dreadful! After all, if he wasn't Jack Fortune, courageous explorer – then who was he?

CHAPTER NINE

The Valley of Flowers

Jack decided to set himself a challenge. Much as he would have liked to stay as far away from the edge as he possibly could, he forced himself to walk in the middle. Sometimes, he even forced himself to go right to the edge and glance over it – casually, as if he just wanted to look at the view. He wasn't sure if it was doing any good or not, but he thought it was worth a try.

All the same, he was very relieved when Sonam led them down a path to the right, which led into another, much smaller valley. Uncle Edmund's eyes lit up.

"Ah! A lateral valley. This is most promising, Jack. The valley is likely to be sheltered from the winds which race through the larger valley, so more delicate plants will be able to grow here. We must keep our eyes peeled."

A narrow stream tumbled down on its way to meet the Dalpo, and beside it grew pink, yellow and purple flowers. Jack thought they were pretty, but his uncle hardly spared them a glance.

"Look, Jack – look up there!" he breathed. The steep banks of the stream were covered with large bushes and trees. Their leaves were dark and glossy. But they were just a backdrop. The real show was the flowers, great frothy clusters made up of individual florets in shades of gold, apricot, crimson, pink, lilac and white. Even Jack, who wouldn't have given even the showiest flower a second glance back in Little Stinchcombe, stared in admiration.

"What are they?" he asked.

"They're rhododendrons, Jack. *Rhodos*, meaning rose, and *dendron*, meaning tree. Not that they're anything to do with the rose family, of course…"

"Oh! But that's just what you're looking for, isn't it?" said Jack, remembering what his uncle had told him just before they left Hakkim.

"That's right," said Uncle Edmund, carefully scanning the slopes, "and these are marvellous. But what I don't yet see… is a blue one."

Jack looked at his uncle in astonishment. All these beautiful colours, and he was complaining because there wasn't a blue one?

"But wouldn't people like to have these in their gardens?" he asked. "I'm sure I would, if I had a garden!"

Uncle Edmund laughed. "Yes, Jack, you're quite right – of course they would. I'm asking too much. These will do very well – at least for the time being. I must get to work." He frowned. "But there's so much to do, I hardly know where to start! Cuttings, seeds, flowers to press – observations to make – and all these different species to draw..."

Jack thought for a bit. Uncle Edmund had helped him on the ladder. Now here was something he could do in return. Never mind about whether he wanted to be an artist or not, he knew he could draw – and he knew that, right here, right now, this was something really useful he could do for Uncle Edmund. He made up his mind. "I'll help," he announced. "I'll draw them. In fact, I won't just draw them, I'll paint them too, and then you'll be able to show people all the colours."

Uncle Edmund's smile lit up his face. "Will you really? Why, that's wonderful, Jack – it'll be such a help! Well then – let's get on!"

Jack rummaged in his father's bag for pencils and paints. This was official expedition work, so he decided to use a new sketchbook from the stores, rather than the one that had belonged to his father.

"We need detail," said his uncle. "Detail and clarity. Draw everything you see, Jack. It's all important." Then he rushed off to tell his assistants what he needed them to do, and left Jack in peace.

Jack saw that each large flower was actually made up of lots of small ones, each with five flouncy petals and long, slender stamens. They were very complicated flowers, and he needed to keep the lines as clear and pure as he could, so that he would be able to show each detail. He realized it would take too long to paint them as well, so he contented himself with mixing up the colours from his father's old paintbox and painting little squares of colour for reference. He hadn't done much painting before, and it was difficult to get the colours right, but he experimented until he got as close a match as he could.

The time passed quickly, and he was surprised when his uncle said it was getting late and they must make camp. He blinked and put his pencil down, suddenly noticing how hungry he was.

"May I?" Uncle Edmund picked up the sketchbook and leafed through it, gazing carefully at each drawing. "You are your father's son, Jack," he said quietly. "You are an artist, as I will never be."

It seemed an odd thing to say. Of course Jack was his father's son. He couldn't get away from that, even if he wanted to.

"I'm not like my father," he said. "I don't want to be."

But he wondered if this was still true. His father was no longer just the person whose fault it was that Jack was an orphan. He was a man with a gift, which Jack now knew he shared. And there was another thing, too: Jack had found out today that he wasn't quite the person he'd thought he was. Perhaps his father wasn't either.

As the evening drew in, the air grew much colder. Sonam and his men gathered armfuls of bamboo and bundles of broad leaves, and soon, instead of just shelters with roofs, they had huts with walls. Jack was delighted.

"Uncle Edmund, come and see," he called. "Sonam's made us a house!"

Uncle Edmund stepped inside and looked round with pleasure. "Oh my word, this is splendid! Sonam's not the friendliest of chaps, but he's very good at what he does, isn't he? This is almost windproof. We'll have no trouble keeping a candle lit tonight, that's for sure. I'll be able to write up my notes in comfort."

But after supper – rice and peppers, as usual – he didn't get his papers out. Instead, he lit his pipe and settled back into his chair with a sigh of pleasure.

"I really feel too tired to do any more tonight," he said. "It's been a good day, but the climb seems to have taken it out of me. My legs aren't as young as yours, Jack."

"You were much better at going up the ladder than I was," said Jack honestly.

Uncle Edmund smiled. "Perhaps. But you did it in the end, didn't you? That's the important thing." His pipe wasn't drawing very well, and he cleaned it out, then packed it with fresh tobacco and relit it. "Ah, that's better." He blew a smoke ring, and watched it wind round the candle and drift away into the night.

"I'll tell you what," he said. "Why don't we have another look at your drawings? They need to be labelled and dated."

Writing wasn't one of Jack's strong points, as Uncle Edmund was well aware from their lessons on board ship. "Hm," he said, watching Jack. "It looks as if a spider crawled through an ink blot and didn't bother to wipe its feet. Look – remember what I told you before. Hold your pen like this, so that it's pointing towards your shoulder. And sit straighter, so that you're looking directly down at the page – practise on a new page, here. Don't press down too hard, just enough to let the ink flow freely. That's right." He watched as Jack wrote. "That's better. Now, keep your small letters to one height, and the large letters to another. Imagine there's a line there to guide you... good, good. All you need to do now is make sure that all the letters lean at the same angle. Consistency, Jack – that's the thing – consistency."

Jack carried on practising while his uncle looked through the drawings he'd done. After a while, he looked at Jack and said, "I meant what I said earlier, Jack. These drawings are good – very good indeed."

Jack wriggled in embarrassment. He wasn't used to compliments – Aunt Constance and Mr Prout hadn't been exactly free with them.

"Yes," continued Uncle Edmund. "You're much better at drawing than I am. But then, that's only to be expected with a father like yours." He looked thoughtful. "You know, Aunt Constance and your grandparents never approved of your father. They felt that Annamaria was wasted on him. They thought she should have married someone with a big house and lots of money. They said she'd thrown herself away, that it was ridiculous to marry for love."

Jack listened. He wanted to hear anything his uncle could tell him about his parents. He knew so little.

"But I always believed they were wrong," his uncle went on. "Matthew was such a colourful character. When he walked into a room, there would be a sort of ripple of excitement – everyone would want to talk to him. He'd been to so many places, done so many things. And Annamaria – she was such a warm, vivid, happy sort of a person. Their whole lives were an adventure…" There was a pause, and Jack leant forward, willing him to go on, to tell him more. "I was never at all like that. Botany has been my great interest and, until now, it's hardly taken me beyond the walls of my laboratory at home, as you know. But when I read the letters that Annamaria sent home, from Paris and Florence, from the Swiss mountains and the Italian lakes – well, I must admit, I often used to wish I had more of Matthew's – what would you call it? – zest for life, I suppose. It's something you have too, Jack."

Jack could feel his heart beating hard in his chest. He wanted to hear more about his father. But then Uncle Edmund started to talk about himself. Jack felt disappointed – but then he felt guilty, because, after all, his uncle had done far more for him than his father ever had. He began to listen again.

"…and then, a few years ago, I heard Sir Joseph Banks speaking for the first time about his travels with Captain Cook. Think of it – he was with Cook on the *Endeavour* when he discovered Terra Australis, the southern continent! It sounded marvellous. But I would never have dreamt I could do anything like that, not until last year."

He fell silent and, after a minute, Jack prompted him. "What happened last year, Uncle?"

His uncle sighed. "Well, I had some bad luck. I sank a good deal of money into an expedition to the southern seas led by Sir Thomas Rivers. The expedition failed. No one returned home, and my money was gone. I had to find a way of restoring my fortunes. At first, I looked for other men to invest in. And then the idea came to me – why not invest in myself? I could do something brave! I didn't have to stay at home for ever, seeing the same people, doing the same things – I could do as Matthew and Annamaria had done, I could follow my heart, be the man I wanted to be, not the man I had become. So you see, I have many reasons for coming on this expedition. Before I left, I thought the most important one was to make money. Now... well, now I'm not so sure."

Uncle Edmund's pipe had gone out again, and he tapped it on the table and loosened the ash, looking a little embarrassed. "Goodness, just listen to me going on. It's late, time for you to get some sleep, Jack. I think I might just step out for a breath of fresh air – I've a bit of a headache..."

Jack put the drawings away in his father's satchel, and curled up under his blankets. As he thought over all that Uncle Edmund had said, it struck him that in the last half-hour he'd learnt more about both his uncle and his father than he ever had before. He felt fonder of both of them.

He lay awake for a while longer. The porters were still sitting round their fire, and he could hear the rise and fall of their voices and an occasional burst of laughter. He felt warm and relaxed, and he suddenly felt that he was exactly where he wanted to be, and with the people he wanted to be with.

He reached for his bag, and traced the initials on the flap. He'd done it so often he didn't need to see them.

"Goodnight, Matthew Percival Fortune," he murmured happily. "Goodnight Annamaria. Sleep tight."

CHAPTER TEN

The Bridge

They stayed among the rhododendrons for three more days. Uncle Edmund was determined to record all the different varieties he could find.

"Marvellous, marvellous," he murmured at the end of their last day's work. "So many wonderful new plants!"

"But no blue one," pointed out Jack.

His uncle shrugged. "Well, it would have been nice. But I could hardly be disappointed, could I? We've achieved a great deal. And who knows what else we shall find before we go home? No, I'm pleased with all we've found so far – very pleased indeed."

The next stage of their journey found them back by the river. The gorge had widened out a little, so there was room for a path, but only just, and the spray made it slippery and treacherous. This time it was Uncle Edmund who was struggling – Jack might not have been at his best with heights, but he was sure-footed, whereas his uncle was continually slipping and stumbling.

After a while, the path led to a bridge.

Uncle Edmund looked at it with horror. "Oh no! Oh, surely not! Why, it's made of *grass*!"

Jack could see what he meant. It wasn't a nice solid stone bridge, like the ones at home. In fact it was very far from solid – it was made simply of woven reeds, attached to a framework of rope. Jack gazed in fascinated horror as it swayed gently from side to side.

"It's perfectly safe," Thondup assured them. He ran lightly across it, and then back again. "You see?"

"Hm," said Uncle Edmund doubtfully. "I carry a little more weight than you. I fear I may be the undoing of it."

Thondup shook his head, laughing. "We will all go across, and you will see everything will be well. One of the men will take your pack, and then you will be as light as a feather."

Soon, only Jack and his uncle were left to cross the bridge. Under his uncle's nervous gaze, Jack stepped onto the bridge. He noticed that the others had taken their shoes off, and so he did the same. The spray from the tumbling waters splashed up through the reeds onto his feet, and his toes curled in shock: it was icy cold. He made it across, and then turned and yelled back to his uncle above the roar of the water.

"It's fine! Quite fun, really! But you should take off your shoes – it gives you a better grip."

"Certainly not!" called Uncle Edmund. "An Englishman has his standards!" Then he stepped onto the bridge and began to march very firmly across, making it dip and sway wildly.

It was a funny sight, and everyone was laughing and cheering him on – when, just as he had almost reached the safety of the other bank, something went horribly wrong. One minute he was striding out confidently; the next, both he and the bridge had collapsed into a churning mass of spray and foam.

For a moment, Jack was so shocked he couldn't move. Then he caught sight of his uncle's head bobbing about in the water, and saw that he was clinging desperately to the remains of the bridge. But the river was fast and furious, and it was obvious that soon his uncle would be carried away.

Looking around desperately, Jack saw a coil of rope lying on the ground where the porters had put their packs down. He grabbed it and wrapped one end round his waist several times, knotting it tightly.

"Get the other end!" he shouted to Thondup, and ran to the edge of the river.

"No!" called Thondup, horrified. "Jack, wait!"

Jack had seen a small rocky spur jutting into the river on a level with the spot where his uncle's head was bobbing up and down in the turbulent water. Slipping and sliding on the wet rocks, he crawled to the end. He could almost reach him – he was so close!

He looked round desperately and saw a branch floating swiftly down the river. He lunged for it, willing himself to reach it, almost losing his balance, but not quite. He managed to grab hold of it and thrust it out across the water towards his uncle.

"Grab this, Uncle! Hold tight!" he shouted.

His uncle's arms thrashed weakly, but he managed to do it. He let the remnant of the bridge go and clung on to the branch. Jack tried to reel him in, but it was too awkward and his feet were slipping on the wet rock, and for a moment he thought he was going to lose his grip completely.

Then suddenly there was someone beside him. Jack caught a glimpse of turquoise close to his face and realized it was Sonam, taking the weight of the branch, holding it steady, so that Jack had a hand free to stretch out to his uncle; somehow, between them, they hauled him up onto the rock. Then Sonam untied the rope from Jack's waist and fastened it round his own. Someone had the other end on the bank, and Sonam pulled it taut, so that it formed a tightrope across the short distance between the rock and the bank. Then he gestured to Jack, who, understanding what he meant, fastened his uncle's hands round the rope.

"Go, Uncle, go!"

His uncle groaned but, with agonizing slowness, managed to pull himself, hand by hand, over the short distance to safety. Then Jack followed, with a gasp of shock as his legs went into the freezing cold water. Finally Sonam balanced himself on the rock, and made what seemed an impossible leap to the bank.

It was over; they were cold and exhausted – but safe.

They huddled in blankets until gradually they stopped shivering. By this time the sun had risen high in the sky and, once they'd changed into dry clothes, Jack felt much better, but he was anxious about his uncle. He'd been in the water much the longest. But he insisted that he was fit to carry on.

"Thanks to you and Sonam, I'm perfectly all right," he said. He paused, then went on gruffly. "But before we go on… well, I'd be dead now if it wasn't for you two. So… thank you. I couldn't be more fortunate in my choice of travelling companions."

Thondup translated for Sonam, who looked embarrassed and awkward. What a decent fellow he was, Jack thought; he obviously didn't like the fuss. Jack tried to look modest too, but it was difficult because, actually, he was bursting with pride. At last, he'd shown himself to be a worthy member of the expedition!

But Thondup was frowning. "Mr Pascoe – that bridge should not have broken. All the rest of us crossed with perfect safety. I have examined the rope which attached the bridge to the tree, and see?" He showed them a length of rope. "This is where it broke. It is not frayed. It has been cut."

Uncle Edmund frowned. "Why, Thondup – what are you saying?"

"This was not an accident. It was deliberate. Mr Pascoe – someone has tried to kill you."

They all stared at the rope. Sonam's face had darkened. Jack could see that he was angry. Of course he was – he wouldn't want to think that any of his men could do such a thing.

"But – why? Why on earth would anyone want to kill *me*?" said Uncle Edmund, bewildered. "These are all splendid fellows! I really can't believe it!"

Thondup shrugged. "Regretfully, the evidence is there. We must consider what is to be done. I will speak with Sonam."

He drew the guide away, and they talked together in low voices.

Uncle Edmund pulled a face. "I don't believe it," he said. "I just don't. There must be some other explanation. I think Thondup is letting his imagination run away with him. It simply doesn't make sense." He stood up and stretched. "Let's be on our way. Do you know, I feel quite invigorated! There's nothing like a cold bath – though I wouldn't choose to have one again in *quite* those circumstances, I must confess!"

Before long, the path began to climb away from the river again. For the time being at least, there were no more spindly ladders or wobbly bridges, but it was hard going for all that, and Jack was glad when they stopped for a rest.

They were well away from the jungle now, and he looked at the view with pleasure. Ranges of white-capped mountains marched away into the distance. Nearby were belts of dark fir trees. They were not far from the snowline now, and sharp blue shadows threw steep crags and cliffs into relief. Jack wondered if anything could possibly live up among the peaks – plants or animals.

He turned to ask his uncle, who had fallen behind, but saw straight away that something was wrong. Uncle Edmund was bending over, his hands on his knees, and Thondup, Sonam and several of the porters were clustered round him, looking worried. Jack ran back down the path.

"Uncle... Uncle, what's wrong?" His breathing sounded ragged and hoarse, and his skin was waxy pale.

"Just a little… short of breath," he wheezed. "Be fine in… in just a minute."

Jack hovered anxiously. Was it because of the accident? Was he ill?

Thondup glanced at him. "Come," he said, "take your uncle's other arm. Let us help him to sit down."

Sonam produced a bamboo container and passed it to Thondup, who nodded and offered it to Uncle Edmund.

"Drink this, Mr Pascoe. It will help you."

Uncle Edmund sniffed and wrinkled his nose.

"What's that?" asked Jack curiously.

"It is called *arak*," said the prince. "It will make him feel stronger."

Uncle Edmund mopped his forehead with his handkerchief and took the flask. "Well, I could certainly do with a little help," he said grimly. He tipped it up and drank steadily. Sonam and the porters watched. At first their faces were anxious, but as he kept drinking they began to grin and nod their heads in admiration.

"Perhaps that is enough," said Thondup hastily. "Arak is a strong drink for those who are not accustomed to it."

"What?" Uncle Edmund's cheeks looked pinker already. He tried to stand up, but wobbled and sat down again. "Oh, my goodness me. Yes, I see what you mean. But I do feel better, to be sure – much better. I don't know what came over me; I suddenly felt queasy, very queasy indeed."

Thondup looked grave. "It is the mountain sickness, Mr Pascoe. It is because we are so high up."

"Oh? But why does no one else feel ill?"

Thondup shrugged. "I do not know. It affects some people more than others. And it affects those most who are unaccustomed to the mountains."

"But I feel all right," pointed out Jack, "and I'm not accustomed to the mountains."

"You are younger. Perhaps this is the reason."

Sonam said something to Thondup, who nodded.

"Sonam believes we are climbing too high and too fast for you. We must go more slowly and rest more often."

Uncle Edmund listened. He looked very tired. He gazed longingly at the mountains stretching northwards. "But then it will take longer. My funds are limited. If we go more slowly, we shall not be able to go as far." He smiled weakly at Jack. "Mathematics in action, dear boy."

Jack watched as Thondup and Sonam spoke again. He wished he could understand what they were saying. He suddenly felt very aware of just how far they were from Little Stinchcombe, and this time the thought was not exciting so much as worrying. Sonam was making a point – that was clear – and he seemed to feel very strongly about it. Thondup listened, then translated.

"Sonam insists that we should return. The sickness is very serious, he says. If we continue, you put your life at risk. He is an experienced guide, Mr Pascoe. You must consider his advice."

Uncle Edmund looked thoughtful. "You said it has come on because of how high we are. Then surely, if we go lower, it will improve. Please tell Sonam that, at the first opportunity, we should take a lower path. In the meantime, we shall go more slowly." He raised his head and looked towards the mountains beyond. "I have not travelled thousands of miles to be defeated by a touch of sickness. We have found beautiful plants already. But there are more, I am convinced of it. This is the chance of a lifetime for me – the chance to do something that matters. I will not give up. I will not turn back."

Jack stared at his exhausted uncle. He might not look much like a hero, but inside, where it counted, he was the bravest person Jack had ever met.

CHAPTER ELEVEN

Disaster!

It wasn't long before Sonam found a path that led downhill. Jack watched his uncle anxiously. The colour slowly came back into his cheeks, and when he praised the "exquisite shape" of a perfectly ordinary-looking pine tree, Jack breathed a sigh of relief. Uncle Edmund was definitely on the mend.

Then Jack saw something much more exciting than a tree. Farther down the path was a village, with gaily painted red houses. Large black animals grazed in the nearby fields.

"Thondup, look! What are those?"

Thondup followed his pointing finger and his eyes lit up. "Ah! This must be Watang! Excellent – we should be able to buy fresh food here… those are yaks, Jack. We spoke of them before, I think."

Jack remembered the chai and winced. "Oh yes."

Fresh food sounded good. They'd had rice, peppers and onions every evening recently – he was longing for a change.

"Our first village!" said Uncle Edmund. "A pretty-looking place. There, you see – if we hadn't had to take a different path to the one we intended, we should never have come across it. The Lord moves in mysterious ways…"

"Indeed," said Thondup with a slight frown. "It has puzzled me for some time that Sonam has not led us to other villages. It was always meant that we should buy food as we went along, and yet we have not done so."

At that point, Sonam came up to speak to Thondup, who listened and nodded.

"Sonam will go down ahead of us to talk to the headman and arrange to buy food," he said.

"Excellent!" said Uncle Edmund. "Then we shall feast tonight!"

But Sonam shook his head when he met them as they approached the village.

"The headman regrets, but it is early in the growing season and the villagers have no food to spare," Thondup told them apologetically.

"Oh. Well, surely there will be other villages?" said Uncle Edmund.

"Yes. Yes, of course."

But Jack could see that the prince was worried. "It'll be all right, won't it, Thondup?" he said when his uncle was out of earshot.

"I hope so. But if we do not find more food, we will not be able to go on for as long as your uncle wishes. I am not sure that he fully understands this. It was never intended that we should carry all the food we needed for the entire expedition."

Jack wasn't sure either. His uncle was the inspiration behind the expedition, but he didn't have much idea about practicalities. He turned back to look regretfully at the village, and noticed that Sonam was talking to someone from the village. There was something odd about the way he was standing, huddled close to a house in the shadow of the overhanging roof, almost as if he didn't want to be seen. He turned to mention it to Thondup, but his friend was already gazing thoughtfully at the guide.

Then Uncle Edmund called to him to point out a particularly brilliant butterfly, and he forgot all about it.

All this talk of food did Jack no good at all. Up till then he'd accepted that on an expedition you just had to put up with boring food. But now, as he plodded on, he began to think longingly of his favourite meals.

"New bread with butter – *cows'* butter – and straw-berry jam," he murmured to himself, licking his lips. "Roast chicken with gravy. Bacon and fried eggs. That rabbit stew that Will's mother makes…" He stopped, struck by a brilliant idea as if by a thunderclap. Why on earth had no one thought of it already? Thondup and Uncle Edmund were walking up ahead, and he ran to catch them up.

"Hunting!" he said breathlessly. "Why don't we hunt for food – or trap it?"

Uncle Edmund looked startled. "Good Heavens, Jack, how bloodthirsty! But yes – I suppose – what do you think, Thondup? I'm afraid I can't really con-tribute myself – there wasn't much call for hunting or trapping in London. Colonel Kydd did suggest I should bring a gun with me, but I confess I have no idea how to use one… oh, look at that now!" He sounded glad of the distraction as he hurried off to inspect a clump of tiny pink flowers growing beside the path.

So *he* was no use. Jack turned to Thondup. "Well?" he said eagerly. "Don't you think it's a good idea?"

The prince smiled. To Jack, it seemed like a distinctly patronizing smile, and he felt a bit cross. Thondup might be older than Jack, but he wasn't a grown-up yet, and Jack didn't appreciate being treated like a child.

"Have you seen very much wildlife that you would care to eat since you came to Changkot?" asked the prince.

Jack thought. There had been leeches, spiders, birds, butterflies, snakes, monkeys… what would monkey stew be like? Hm… well, in any case, he hadn't seen any since they'd left the rainforest behind. Leech soup? Snake steaks?…

"You see? There are not many animals that we can eat. Farther up, we may see a herd of wild sheep from time to time, and then indeed we may be able to kill one. But mostly, for meat, the mountain people use the yak. While it lives, the yak provides milk for cheese and butter, and wool to spin and weave. But it only gives meat once, when it dies."

"So there's nothing else?" asked Jack, disappointed. "Aren't there any wild deer?"

Thondup shook his head. "Not in these parts." Then he paused dramatically. "Of course, there *are* stories of other creatures which are said to live in the mountains."

"Stories? What stories?" said Jack, perking up.

"Oh, it is all nonsense, I expect," said Thondup cheerfully, pushing aside a bramble. "I am sure there is nothing to fear, no matter what people may say."

"But what *do* they say?" said Jack, intrigued.

"What? You want to know? Oh, but they are travellers' tales, nothing more."

"Thondup!"

"Oh well, if you really *do* want to know…"

"Of course I do!" If this had been Will Puddy, Jack would have knocked him down and given him a good pummelling by now. Thondup laughed and held up his hands to admit defeat.

"We have not reached the snowline yet," he began. "If we do – if your uncle is well enough – you will see that beyond is a place of ice, snow and rock. The cold is so bitter that your breath freezes as it comes out of your mouth, and if you do not take care, your fingers lose all feeling and turn black. Your eyelashes are coated with ice. The snow deceives you – everything is white, so every direction looks the same. Your mind becomes frozen and numb, and soon you begin to be uncertain whether the things you think you see are real – or just dreams walking.

"I think this may be what has happened in the case of those who come down from the high places with stories of the *metoh-kangmi*. But who knows? Who can tell what may live in the wild places where the eyes of men seldom reach?"

"The *metoh-kangmi*?" Jack repeated, fascinated. "What are they?"

Thondup gazed towards the horizon, where mountain peaks melted into mist. "In truth, there is little to relate," he continued. "Only stories of a figure beyond the usual height of men."

"So it's a monster?" prompted Jack.

"A monster? No. There is a spirit that dwells behind their eyes, as there is behind a man's. They are said to be enormously strong. Though how anyone knows all this – since they live, if they live at all, in the remotest places and shun the presence of men – I cannot tell. They are said to be the guardians of the sacred places. I know of a man who ventured onto Mount Zemu. He did not believe the stories of the guardians, and wished to prove them false."

"What happened?" said Jack, his eyes like saucers.

"He was never seen or heard of again. The priests from the monastery went out in search of him, but they found nothing."

"Nothing?"

Thondup paused dramatically. "Nothing. Except – a set of giant footprints in the snow."

As he spoke, Sonam, who was walking nearby, glanced at Thondup and murmured something to him. Thondup nodded gravely.

"What did he say?" asked Jack.

Thondup shrugged. "Sonam heard me mention the *metoh-kangmi*, and reminded me of a legend – a foolish one, I have no doubt."

"Well?" demanded Jack. "What is it?"

"It is said that the sighting of one of these creatures – the *metoh-kangmi* – will be followed by death."

Thondup smiled. "I suppose that may explain why so few people have ever seen one."

Jack shivered, wondering if it was true.

"What does it mean, '*metoh-kangmi*'?"

"It means 'wild men of the snow'."

Jack began to feel excited. The *metoh-kangmi* sounded much more exciting than a blue rhododendron. Perhaps he could capture one, and they could take it back to England and present it to the King. He pictured the scene. He and Uncle Edmund would lead the great beast down the gangplank. Bands would be playing, and King George himself would congratulate them. Aunt Constance would be weeping with pride... oh, he could see it all!

He entertained himself for the rest of that day's trek with schemes for catching the creature, and that night he asked Uncle Edmund if he had heard of the *metoh-kangmi*. His uncle frowned.

"It reminds me of something... what was it now? Why yes – that's it! Do you remember the tale Colonel Kydd told us, when we were in the botanic garden? He said that if there is a blue rhododendron anywhere, it might be in a hidden valley on a holy mountain, which—"

"Which had some kind of guardian!" breathed Jack.

"And he said he thought the name of the mountain began with a Z. I wonder... could it be?..."

"Zemu!"

They looked at each other. Could it be? Were they so close to the hidden valley – if, indeed it really existed? Could the blue rhododendron be within their reach?

"But we can't go to Zemu," said Jack sorrowfully, his dreams fading fast. "We promised the Maharaja."

"Yes," sighed his uncle. "We did." He paused. "But perhaps it's worth just mentioning again to Thondup. Just in case..."

So they did. But Thondup was adamant. Mount Zemu was sacred. It didn't matter how many blue rhododendrons there might be on the holy mountain, it was forbidden, and that was that. And anyway, there was the guardian – the mountain was dangerous. They could not, must not go there.

"Well, well," yawned Uncle Edmund. "Let's leave it at that. I'm very pleased with the progress we've made so far – we have some very fine specimens. But I must confess I would dearly love to find that blue rhododendron. It's easy to forget about such things as money troubles out here – but they do exist. And there's no doubt that such a plant as that would be a swift way to fame and fortune. But there it is. If we can't go to Zemu, we can't. And we certainly have lots of other really terrific plants. Yes, I'm certain we shall make a considerable stir when we return to England, Jack. Sir Joseph Banks will certainly wish to have some of our specimens for Kew. Why, His Majesty King George himself will surely take an interest…"

Uncle Edmund clearly accepted that Mount Zemu was out of bounds, and so did Jack. They'd promised the Maharaja, and a promise was a promise. But that night his sleep was disturbed by dreams. Tall creatures with shaggy golden fur stood guarding the entrance to a secret valley. As Jack and his uncle approached, they could see trees covered in flowers of an exquisite blue. Uncle Edmund gasped in delight. But the monsters growled fiercely and gnashed their teeth. Their hooked claws came within an inch of raking Jack's face, and he backed away, convinced he was about to die…

Jack's eyes flew open and he sat bolt upright. Something was wrong. It was dark, the grey darkness that comes just before dawn. The camp should have been quiet, but it wasn't. He could hear shouts, thumps, bellows – bellows? What on *earth* was going on? He sprang off his campbed and stumbled outside – to find himself staring into the eyes of a huge black head topped with massive horns.

Jack backed carefully into the tent, pinching himself just to make absolutely sure he wasn't still dreaming. "Uncle!" he said in a loud, urgent whisper. "There's a bull outside our tent!"

"Hm? What's that?" said his uncle, propping himself up on one elbow and fumbling for his glasses. "Is this one of your jokes, Jack?"

The great head poked through the tent flap, and a pair of mild dark eyes gazed at them tenderly. Round the creature's neck hung a scarlet halter, decorated with tiny bells which tinkled sweetly.

"Why, it's a yak!" exclaimed Uncle Edmund. "What on earth is a yak doing in our tent? Shoo! Go on, shoo!"

Confronted by Uncle Edmund prancing about like a maniac, the yak hastily withdrew. But its horns caught in the blanket which formed the roof of the tent. The ridge pole collapsed and the blanket wrapped itself round the beast's head and shoulders. It bellowed in fear and twisted and turned, trying to free itself. Uncle Edmund threw himself protectively on top of the bag which contained his precious instruments and notebooks, and Jack waved his arms and shouted to frighten the yak away.

In the dim light of dawn, as he scrambled to his feet and untangled himself from the tent, Jack could see that there were other yaks too. Several of the great beasts were thundering round the campsite, obviously panicked by the men who were shouting at them, trying to drive them away from the tents. Some of the porters had grabbed sticks and branches from the scattered ashes of last night's fire; Jack did the same, and they formed a semicircle and gradually began to herd the yaks away from the campsite.

Once the confused creatures were well away from the camp, Jack left the others to it and hurried back. Uncle Edmund was gazing round at the chaos. He looked bewildered.

"Well," he said. "That was exciting, wasn't it? Poor creatures – they must have been terrified."

"They weren't the only ones," said Jack. "I've never had such a shock in my life! They've made a bit of a mess, haven't they?" But as he looked around he realized that this was an understatement. The campsite was a shambles. There wasn't a tent left standing. Every single one had been trampled to the ground.

Then he saw something even worse.

"What is it?" asked his uncle, peering round. "There aren't any more, are there?"

"No... no," stammered Jack. "But... but look."

Every night, the porters carefully arranged all the packs under a shelter, to protect them in case of rain. But now, the branches which had formed the supports had been knocked to one side or lay on the ground. The heavy canvas bags had been torn apart, and their contents were scattered. Rice, vegetables and meal had been ground into the earth. Torn plant papers and petals drifted gently about the clearing, and carefully labelled boxes which had contained precious seed had been smashed. Notebooks lay open, their pages muddy and torn.

Uncle Edmund walked over slowly, and picked up a book. He smoothed the paper absently with his fingers, and gazed around in bewilderment.

Jack couldn't bear it. They had come so far and done so much, and now, in the space of a few incomprehensible minutes, it had all been destroyed. He started to sift frantically through the rubbish – surely something must be left!

Thankfully, he found that some of the food bags were almost undamaged; a few seed boxes and cuttings had survived, and of course his uncle's most recent notebook was safe in his bag, as were most of Jack's drawings.

But that was all. Everything else was ruined.

Thondup appeared at Jack's side. He held one of the bags in his hands.

"These bags," he said quietly. "They have been cut. See? With a knife. Like at the bridge. This was no accident. I will be back soon. Take care of your uncle." He looked at Uncle Edmund, stumbling through the chaos like a grey ghost. "He will need you now."

It was a couple of hours before Thondup returned. In the meantime, Jack had persuaded his uncle to start tidying up and repacking what they were able to save.

Uncle Edmund did as he suggested, but it was clear that his heart wasn't in it.

"There seems little point," he said heavily. "We might as well face it, Jack. Everything's gone. We're finished."

Jack's thoughts raced. There must be a way through – they couldn't simply give up. "Couldn't we just collect everything again?" he asked eagerly.

His uncle shook his head wearily. "We're running out of time. I cannot afford to keep the porters on for any longer than we planned – and we haven't enough food, or the means to store the specimens." He picked up a crushed seed box, and let it fall from his fingers. "It's all been for nothing, Jack. That's the sad truth of it. I've failed. It's over."

Jack gazed at his uncle miserably. For once, he could think of nothing to say.

Then Thondup returned, looking tense and serious. He drew them aside, so that no one else could hear what he had to say. "It is as I feared. The yaks were let loose deliberately and brought here to cause destruction. I followed their trail back to the village from which they came. It is a small hamlet with only a few houses. I spoke to the people there. It appears that one of the villagers woke in the night, thinking he heard a noise in the yak field. The moon was bright, and he saw a man moving amongst the animals. By the time he reached the field, it was too late – they were gone. But he recalled that in the moonlight he had seen a flash of turquoise – an earring." He paused, and looked at them. "Who do you know who has a turquoise earring?"

Jack frowned. The only person he could think of who wore a turquoise earring was Sonam. *Sonam*? "No!" he said. "It can't be!" Not Sonam, who had guided them all this way – who had taught him so much and had helped him to rescue Uncle Edmund. He'd admired him so much!

Thondup looked at him sadly. "Who else? I have suspected him for some time now."

"But – why? Why would he do such a thing? It can't be true – not Sonam!"

"I think the Dewan is behind it. It was he who employed Sonam. My father believes the Dewan to be a loyal servant, but I think he is loyal only to himself. He is greedy, he is arrogant and he hates the British. That may be reason enough – or there may be something more, some secret enterprise of his own. I do not know."

"But – at the bridge – he saved my life! Well, he and Jack between them." said Uncle Edmund, looking bewildered.

"This is true, and it has puzzled me. Perhaps the Dewan forced him in some way – perhaps, after cutting the rope, he could not bear to see the consequences of his action. I do not know. But he is certainly responsible for what happened here. I think we must confront him," said Thondup.

"But – if it's true, what do you think he will do?" A frightening thought came into Jack's head. If Sonam was capable of planning to kill Uncle Edmund at the bridge – even if he had changed his mind at the last minute – how would he respond to being accused? Thondup touched the long curved knife he always carried at his side.

"My father is no particular friend of the British. But he gave you and your uncle permission to travel in Hakkim. I will not allow him to be dishonoured and defied in this way. Do not fear, Jack."

Jack stared at him. Most of the time he forgot all about Thondup being a prince. He was just his friend – sometimes a bit annoying, but generally good company and fun. But now there was something in his face that showed another side to him. He expected to be obeyed.

He snapped out orders to four of the porters, who looked startled, but went off quickly to do his bidding. Within minutes, they returned, dragging a startled-looking Sonam between them.

Jack could not understand the words that passed between them. But it was easy to read in Sonam's face what he was feeling. First he looked defiant. Then, as Thondup spoke, and showed him the neatly cut piece of rope from the bridge and pointed to his earring, his shoulders slumped and he put his hands over his eyes, as if he couldn't bear to look at them. Then he began to talk.

"It is as I thought," Thondup told them when he had finished. "The Dewan gave him instructions to – how can I put it? – make your expedition fail."

"To sabotage it, you mean?" said Uncle Edmund, looking distressed. "Good Heavens!"

"Yes. So the bridge – that was his work. Also the yaks, as we know. And he arranged for the headman at Watang and other places not to sell food to us." Thondup looked angry. "When we thought he was asking for food, he was in fact doing exactly the opposite – he was threatening or bribing the villagers to deny us what we needed. How did I not see? Why did I not speak to these people myself? Oh, I am very much to blame!"

Uncle Edmund looked concerned. "No, no indeed, my dear prince! You are no more to blame than I – I had no idea at all – I never suspected a thing!"

Jack said nothing. He felt hugely disappointed. He had trusted Sonam – he'd liked him! And all this time he'd been an enemy. It didn't bear thinking about.

"But what still puzzles me," went on Uncle Edmund, "is *why* the Dewan went to so much trouble to stop us?"

Thondup glanced at him. "He distrusts the British. He is not alone in that. And he was angry, because he had spoken against your expedition, and you were able to persuade my father to change his mind. This he perhaps regarded as a slight, an insult." He paused. "This may not console you, but Sonam says that, as he grew to know you, Mr Pascoe – and Jack – he became very sorry for what he had been forced to do. But the Dewan has a hold over him. Sonam has a daughter whom he loves dearly. She has been very ill, and the Dewan promised to provide food and doctors for her. But only if Sonam would follow his orders."

Uncle Edmund looked angry. "George Inchmore was right about that fellow – he *is* a bounder! But now we must consider our next step… I suppose we have no alternative but to return to Changkot by the short-est route possible, and hope that, without Sonam's interference, we will be able to buy food on the way. Unless…"

"Unless what, Uncle?" asked Jack. His uncle's face had suddenly lit up. But there was something else there too: something calculating, something that was almost greedy. He'd never seen such a look on his uncle's face before, and he didn't like it.

"Well, it just occurs to me," said Uncle Edmund slowly, "that there may be a way to salvage something from all this. Perhaps, after all, it is not necessary to go back to England empty-handed."

"What do you mean?" asked Jack, puzzled.

Uncle Edmund looked at them both, his eyes shining with excitement.

"We must search for the hidden valley. We must go to Mount Zemu and find the blue rhododendron. Don't you see? It's the only way to save the expedition!"

Chapter Twelve

The Sacred Mountain

Jack hardly dared to look at Thondup. He couldn't believe his uncle had even thought of such a thing, let alone suggested it. He opened his mouth to speak, but the prince got in first. His eyes flashed with anger.

"Impossible!" he said. "No one is allowed on Mount Zemu. It is sacred. You know this, sir. It was the condition set by my father and agreed by you – that you should not set foot on our holy places. And Zemu is the holiest of them all."

"Yes, yes, of course I know all that," said Uncle Edmund testily. "And I was fully prepared to respect your laws. But now – everything has changed, don't you see? The rest of my life depends on whether I make a success of my time here – it matters that much. Forgive me for reminding you of it, but it is thanks to the man indirectly recommended by your father that I stand to lose everything I've worked for. My one chance – my *only* chance – is to find the hidden valley. If the stories are true, that is where we will find the blue rhododendron. And if I can find the blue rhododendron – why, that will change my life! We are so close – *so* close!" He turned to gaze at the peaks of the holy mountain, glittering and lovely in the cold sunlight.

Thondup looked grave. "The stories may not be true. But even if they are, it does not alter the truth. You may not go there. It is forbidden." He paused. "And do not forget that the mountain is guarded."

"Guarded? Oh, you mean by this mysterious monster that you and Kydd told us about. Surely you don't believe such ridiculous stories!" scoffed Uncle Edmund.

"Stories are often true. It is certainly true that people have disappeared in circumstances which cannot be easily explained. As I have told you, giant footprints have been clearly seen in the snow. But all this is – how do you say it? – beside the point. You may not tread on Zemu, because it is sacred – and because you promised my father that you would respect his word on this."

Jack looked from one to the other. Thondup was determined. But so was Uncle Edmund. There was a strained, hectic look about him; he didn't look like himself at all. Jack felt torn between the two of them.

"Please," he burst out, "Uncle, don't be like this. We gave the Maharaja our word – we *promised*!" He pictured the man in the simple robe, with the merry smile and the room in the sky, and felt miserable. How could they face him again, if they broke their word?

"I'm sorry, Jack, but I must and will go," said Uncle Edmund stiffly. "I've made my decision, and there's an end of it."

Thondup was silent for a moment. When he spoke, his voice was as chilly as the snow-capped mountains. "I will do this much. I will take you to the monastery at the foot of Mount Zemu. There you may put your case to the Abbot and seek his permission to go onto the mountain. But I am certain he will not give it.

"And now I will send Sonam and most of the porters back to Changkot. We do not need many men to carry the little that is left of our baggage."

After he'd gone, Jack looked at his uncle unhappily. Uncle Edmund sighed. "I know, Jack – I know. I don't like it either. But what other way is there? You know how much is at stake! And these stories about a god on a mountain, and a guardian – it's all just silly nonsense and superstition – you must realize that."

"It's their country," said Jack stubbornly. "Surely they know what's in it better than we do?"

His uncle turned away. "This is nonsense," he said flatly. "I've made my mind up and that's it. Get yourself ready to leave."

Jack felt miserable. He couldn't believe how quickly everything had changed. Yesterday, everything was going so well. Now, nothing was.

Before Sonam left for Changkot, he came to see Jack and Uncle Edmund. He looked troubled, and he bowed deeply.

"Sonam asks me to tell you that he deeply regrets what he was made to do," translated Thondup. "He says that he hopes your endeavours will be crowned with success. And to you, Jack, he says you are brave like a lion, and he wishes he had a son like you. And he asks your forgiveness."

Uncle Edmund hesitated, then nodded reluctantly. But Jack felt sorry for the guide. It wasn't his fault that he was poor and the Dewan was a bully. He'd done what he had to do to be a good father. On impulse, Jack stuck his hand out. Sonam looked puzzled, as if he didn't quite know what to do with it, and then shyly took hold of it. He smiled, and stood up straighter. Then he thought of something. He reached into a pouch fastened onto his belt, and brought out an oval-shaped piece of polished turquoise – a smaller version of his earring.

"He wishes to give this to you," said Thondup, look-ing a little surprised. "It was to have been a gift for his daughter, but he hopes now that it will bring good fortune to you."

Jack was embarrassed. "Oh, I can't take that," he said, "not if it was for his daughter."

But Sonam insisted, and finally Jack gave in and stowed it carefully in his father's bag. Sonam put his hands together and bowed, and then he and most of the porters set off.

Jack, Uncle Edmund, Thondup and the porters who were left turned towards Mount Zemu. There was no chatter that day. The porters were clearly on edge, and Uncle Edmund and Thondup spoke little and avoided each other. Jack trudged along unhappily.

Later they huddled round the campfire, sipping tea that tasted of smoke and gazing up at the masses of stars, brilliant pinpricks in the black night sky.

"We are closer to the stars here than we could ever be in England," said Uncle Edmund quietly to Jack. "You'd almost think that if you reached out you could simply pluck one from the sky and hold it in your hand."

Jack didn't answer. He thought about a handful of starlight. What would it feel like? Would it be hot, like fire, or cold, like ice? Would glittering sparks dart and dance, or would it lie still, like a little pool in the basin of his hand?

He remembered the piece of turquoise, and took it out. Tiny golden veins gleamed in the firelight. He thought about Sonam and his uncle. He didn't know much about the stars, but then again he wasn't sure he knew all that much about people either. Sonam had seemed to be one person, then he'd turned out to be another, and now he was back to how he'd seemed in the first place. And Uncle Edmund – what about him? Back in England, he'd seemed to be one person. Out here, he'd turned into someone else – someone Jack could admire, someone he'd become very fond of. But now? Now, he wasn't so sure.

It had been a long day and he felt very tired. As he went to his tent, he paused and looked back at the campfire. Uncle Edmund and the others were looming black shapes that blotted out the stars. Jack shivered and felt lonely. At that moment, he would even have been pleased to see Aunt Constance. At least he always knew where he stood with her.

The next day, they came to a fork in the path. The left fork went straight on, the one on the right led to the monastery at Dilphut. Thondup called a halt, then turned and looked at Uncle Edmund. They had hardly spoken since the morning before.

"I ask you again, Mr Pascoe," said Thondup, "will you change your mind? You could collect more plants on the way back to Changkot, and indeed there are many beautiful flowers close to the city. Please – respect Zemu, remember your word to my father. Think of your own safety, and that of Jack – and turn away."

With an impatient shake of his head, Uncle Edmund refused. "My mind is set on this, Thondup. If the Abbot refuses – well, I shall have to think again. But I know – I just know – that the hidden valley is there. It's like a quest, do you see? When I find the valley, I shall find my heart's desire – I know it!"

Jack was beginning to wonder if his uncle's mountain sickness had come back and was affecting his brain – he was certainly saying some very strange things.

Thondup looked down and said nothing. Then he turned away and led them along the path to Dilphut.

The path crawled up between steep precipices. An ice-cold wind howled down the narrow pass. It sounded like a ghostly voice, and the men looked round uneasily. Neither Thondup nor Uncle Edmund had spoken a word since they'd left the main path, not even to Jack, and he felt lonely and miserable. He felt sure that something very bad was about to happen, and he wished desperately that he could find a way to make everything come right again. He was very fond of his uncle, and of Thondup too. Why must they be at odds? Why couldn't his uncle see how wrong he was?

That night, they camped on a slope at the base of a rock face. It was bitterly cold. Fortunately, George Inchmore had made them pack sheepskin coats for when it got colder. Jack felt guilty when he remembered how they'd scoffed, unable to imagine such cold in the warmth of Changkot. But even though he kept his coat on and huddled under extra blankets, he still couldn't get warm. He thought regretfully of Sonam: he would have constructed something better than these flimsy tents to sleep in. The wind wailed and moaned like a living thing, and underneath it was another noise, a rumbling, threatening sound, as if the mountain itself was waking and growling in anger. Eventually Jack managed to drift off, but a huge stone lion prowled through his dreams, lifting its giant paws to crush anything in its path, moving closer... and closer... and even closer...

Then suddenly it was on top of him, and he snapped awake to find that the night was being torn apart. Jagged streaks of lightning ripped through the sky, and thunder roared its fury. But there was another sound too, the same grinding, growling noise he'd noticed a few hours earlier. It was much louder now. Confused and frightened by the din, he stumbled out of the tent to see what was happening, dimly aware that his uncle was somewhere behind him.

Sharp darts of hail and snow stung his skin, but much worse than this was the fact that the mountain itself seemed to be on the move. Stones and pebbles hurtled past him, and a splinter of rock tore his cheek open. He tasted blood in his mouth, and for a second he stood shocked, unable to move. Then someone grabbed his arm and pulled him towards the foot of the cliff. It was Thondup. Stumbling and scrambling over the shifting stones, Jack twisted round to see where his uncle was – and saw to his horror that he was directly in the path of a huge falling rock.

"UNCLE!" screamed Jack. In the space of a second, Uncle Edmund looked up, saw the danger, and threw himself to one side. He very nearly escaped it, but not quite – Jack saw it strike a glancing but savage blow to his leg. His uncle's face, lit briefly by a flash of lightning, was twisted in agony. Jack ran back to him, his feet slipping on the slippery scree. Thondup plunged after him, and between them they managed to half drag, half carry Uncle Edmund to the shelter of the cliff, where they and the porters all huddled miserably to wait out the storm and the night. Jack couldn't stop trembling, and he noticed that even Thondup shuddered from time to time.

When they took stock in the morning, they understood that, bad as it was, it could have been much worse. No one had been killed, and most of them had escaped with cuts and bruises. But Uncle Edmund's leg was in a bad way. It was red and hot to the touch, and very swollen. Gently, Jack eased his uncle's boot off. He soaked pieces of linen in melted snow, and his uncle closed his eyes in relief as the bandages cooled his skin.

"Thank you, Jack, thank you. Oh my goodness... oh dear me, it does hurt, but that definitely helps..." Jack looked at his uncle, concerned. His face was white and drawn, and the skin around his mouth was pinched and puckered in pain.

What were they going to do? Never mind the hidden valley – it was perfectly clear that Uncle Edmund wasn't going to be able to walk *anywhere*. Jack shivered. They were nearing the snowline, and it struck him that the accident could not have happened in a more inhospitable place.

Thondup had been talking to the porters. They looked upset, and when they looked up at the mountain, their faces were full of fear.

"They want to go back," he said grimly. His face was streaked with dust, and a cut ran across one cheek. "They say that we have come too close, that the god is angry and seeks to throw us off the mountain. They would prefer to leave now, without delay, but they have agreed to make a stretcher for Mr Pascoe and take him to the monastery, so that the monks may treat his leg. There also we can ask the monks to pray to the god for us, and beg him to let us depart in safety."

Jack tried to think about all this. Could it really be true that last night's avalanche had been the result of the god's anger?

It was all too difficult, he decided. He was in Thondup's country now, and he would simply do whatever Thondup thought best.

His uncle's eyes flickered open.

"Jack," he said, "would you give me some water?"

Jack did so, and his uncle sipped it gratefully. Then he tried to prop himself up. "Thondup," he said, sounding agitated. "I must speak to Thondup."

Thondup knelt down beside him.

"You must rest," he said gently. Uncle Edmund shook his head wearily.

"Your highness, you are too kind. I am sorry. I have been stubborn and… ungracious… and I was prepared to go back on… on the word I had given to your father." He drank more water, and his voice became a little stronger. "It is my fault we are in this mess, and I am deeply, deeply sorry. I do not know… I do not know what came over me. How could I think of repaying your father for his kindness in this… this dishonourable way? I am in your hands. We shall do as you see fit."

CHAPTER TWELVE

"We will go on to the monastery," said Thondup quietly. "The monks there are skilled in healing. When you are able, we will return to Changkot."

Uncle Edmund closed his eyes again for a moment, his face creased in pain.

"Yes," he said. "That sounds like a plan." Then he turned, searching for Jack. "After all," he said, "we are not returning with nothing. We have… we have found each other, have we not? And if I have lost everything, and we have no choice but to throw ourselves on the mercy of your dear aunt – well, at least it will henceforth be two against one!" He patted Jack's hand, and then leant back, exhausted.

As Jack looked at him, something shifted inside him. His uncle didn't want *that* much, after all: just the chance to go a little further and see if he could find his – what was it he'd called it? – his 'heart's desire'. It was only a flower, after all – it wasn't worth anything to Thondup or his father, but it was worth everything to Uncle Edmund. Jack knew perfectly well that it wasn't just that it might be the means to make his fortune; it would also be the outward proof that he was a better man than he'd thought he was: that he, meek and scholarly Edmund Pascoe, could undertake a tremendous adventure and succeed in it.

He'd achieved so much. He'd travelled thousands of miles, put up with seasickness and mountain sickness, risked death by drowning, tackled rickety bridges and terrifying ladders, been betrayed by Sonam and attacked by yaks – he'd survived all that *and* been burdened with an inconvenient nephew whom he could so easily have left at home – and now he'd lost everything.

Jack felt a strange kind of anger building up inside himself, and before he knew it he'd made a decision. There was nothing more his uncle could do, but that wouldn't stop Jack from doing it for him. He would go on in place of his uncle. *He* would find the hidden valley. If that meant crawling through snow and ice on his hands and knees and risking the fury of a bad-tempered god and a terrifying guardian, then so be it. Uncle Edmund had done more for him than anyone else in his life so far, and now he was going to repay the favour.

He would tell no one – not yet. But when his chance came, he would be ready.

Chapter Thirteen

Dilphut

The porters made a stretcher for Uncle Edmund, but Jack could see that it was very uncomfortable for his poor uncle. The path was uneven, and the first time they stumbled his leg was jolted so badly that he cried out in agony. After that they went more slowly. Jack wanted to help, and he offered to take a turn, but they said it wouldn't work to have two people of different sizes carrying it and, as he could see that this was true, he said no more.

They finally arrived at Dilphut in the afternoon. The monastery was on a sheltered green ridge, but behind it Zemu looked cold and bleak. Rocky overhangs cast sharp, dark shadows across the snow. Jack shivered, and looked back at the monastery.

Along the path, bright prayer flags fluttered on posts and silver bells tinkled. He wondered if the bells sent prayers out to the world, in the way the flags were meant to.

"You'd better send a prayer for me," he muttered, touching one of the bells as they walked past. "I'm going to need all the help I can get."

What would happen if he couldn't persuade the Abbot to allow him onto the mountain? Well, he'd just go anyway, he decided. But how would he find the way? It was a big mountain. How on earth was he to know where the hidden valley was? And, worst of all, what if, after all they'd been through, there *was* no hidden valley? Or if there was a valley, but there was no blue rhododendron? What if the whole thing was no more than a travellers' tale? Don't be silly, he told himself. Of *course* it's true. It *has* to be.

The Abbot would know where it was. But would he be able to persuade the Abbot to help him?

As they walked through the entrance to the monastery, his thoughts were interrupted by a crowd of excited little boys. They all wore dark-orange robes and leggings and had closely shaven heads.

"Who are they?" Jack asked Thondup. "They can't be monks, surely – they're much too little!"

"No, they're not," said Thondup, smiling at the children. "Some of them may become monks one day, but not all. Many boys in Hakkim spend a year or two in a monastery for their education. I did so myself. You must not mind them – they have not seen anyone who looks like you before!"

They clustered eagerly round Jack, peering at his face and trying to touch his curly hair. Jack grinned and reached out in return to pat the soft, dark stubble on top of the nearest boy's head. They all exploded with laughter and pushed their heads towards him to be touched in turn.

Then a hush fell. The boys fell back as a monk came to greet the travellers. He looked quite old – about the same age as Uncle Edmund, Jack thought, or perhaps even older. His face was round and smooth, and his dark eyes were kind and tranquil. He placed his hands together and bowed deeply to Thondup. He looked with interest at Jack, and then with concern at Uncle Edmund.

He listened to Thondup for a few minutes, then spoke to the porters.

"This is Champa," explained Thondup. "He has ordered that your uncle should be taken to the – how do you call it? – the infirmary? A place where his injury can be examined. But for us he offers refreshment, and then he will take us to see the Abbot. Few visitors travel here outside the time of the great festival, he says, so we are all the more welcome." Thondup paused, looking puzzled. "But he tells me a strange thing. He says that there was another visitor here, earlier today. One who hid his face in his robe, as if he did not wish to be known. This stranger asked if a group of travellers had passed through. They answered that none had, and he hastened on his way. I do not understand this. Who could it have been?" He frowned. "Still, let us go. Food – this sounds good – no?"

They were taken to the refectory, where they ate rice and vegetables cooked in a delicious spicy sauce. It felt odd at first to be indoors and with so many other people. With a slight sense of shock, Jack realized that he hadn't been with children his own age since he'd left England, many months before. There had been one or two boys who were part of the crew on board ship, but they had always been busy, and anyway turned their noses up at having anything to do with Jack, who was slightly younger and, worse, a passenger. If they had spent longer in Calcutta, he was sure he would have made friends with the gardener's boys, who lived in the hut at the end of the large garden; but there hadn't been time to work out how to get round Colonel Kydd's rules and regulations, which included not having anything to do with the servants.

He looked around at the boys, all chatting and joking in a language he didn't understand. He felt a bit left out. He would have tried to get to know them, but he was so anxious that he just wanted to get the meal over and see the Abbot and get on with things.

After they'd eaten, they went to see how Uncle Edmund was getting on. Though still pale, he looked much better. His eyes shone with excitement as he told them about an ointment which Champa had smoothed onto his painfully swollen leg, before setting it and fixing it to a splint with bandages.

"You can't imagine how cooling it was – really, the pain and heat just seemed to melt away! Of course, Champa can't speak English and I can't speak Hakkimese – but we got on pretty well with sign language and, as far as I can judge, it seems the monks make the ointment from plants which they grow." He paused. "Plants really are the most wonderful things. I shall never be sorry that I've given my life to studying them, whatever happens – even if I have to go back to England with nothing. Their beauty enchants the eye, their fragrance delights the nose, they feed us and they heal us... they are truly the most marvellous creations! And Champa can teach me so much more about them. And see?" He lifted up two sticks, forked at the top and padded with sheepskin. "Champa has found crutches for me. So I can hobble along with you to speak to the Abbot." He looked seriously at Thondup. "It is my duty to explain myself, and I will – have no fear on that score."

Jack thought Champa must be a remarkably good doctor. He'd not only fixed Uncle Edmund's leg, he seemed to have sorted his head out too. It was good to see him so cheerful again.

Soon they were all crowding into the Abbot's small room. Like the Maharaja's, it was high up, looking out across the monastery to the mountains beyond. The ceiling rested on wooden pillars painted with scarlet, blue, emerald and gold patterns, and on the walls hung fascinating pictures showing monsters with multiple arms or elephant's heads, beautiful girls with dark eyes and red lips, gardens filled with bright flowers and fierce warriors brandishing cruel swords. He thought of the simple pictures of plants he had done for his uncle. It would be much more fun to do pictures like these.

The Abbot was quite small and rather plump, with several chins and a tummy that rested comfortably on his crossed legs. He wore the same tawny orange robes as the other monks. The flesh on his face was creased into wrinkles, but his back, like the Maharaja's, was straight and firm. He smiled at them, spreading his arms wide in greeting, and indicating that, like him, they should sit on the floor – except for Uncle Edmund, who was provided with a chair and a stool on which to rest his leg.

To Jack's surprise, the Abbot spoke English, though not as well as Thondup and his father. Jack felt a bit embarrassed about this. Little Stinchcombe was far less remote than Dilphut, but Jack certainly couldn't imagine anyone there being able to speak to a foreigner in his own language. Well, unless an ancient Roman stumbled by, in which case Mr Prout might manage a word or two in Latin.

The Abbot smiled widely. "The prince, the traveller and his boy," he said. "All are welcome. You have travelled far, I think?"

Uncle bowed clumsily in his chair. "Oh yes, Your... Your Grace," he said. "We are a very long way from home. We have come from England. We have travelled thousands of miles across sea and land."

The Abbot nodded, as if he already knew this. "Indeed, this is very far." He looked at Uncle Edmund quizzically. "And why did you choose to do this? Why have you come to Hakkim, and why to Zemu?"

And there it was. The big question.

How would Uncle Edmund answer?

The whole room seemed to hold its breath as he began to tell the story of the expedition. No one interrupted, although sometimes Thondup helped out when the Abbot couldn't understand.

Finally, he came to the end. The Abbot's face had become serious as Uncle Edmund spoke of Sonam's betrayal and the avalanche. He clasped his hands loosely together and kept his gaze fixed on Jack's uncle. His face was calm again; it was impossible to know what he was thinking. The minutes stretched out before he finally stirred and began to speak.

"You have come very far, Mr Pascoe, to find your dream. And what is that dream? Fame? Fortune? A blue flower? Are these things worth all that you have risked?" Then he looked at Jack, and smiled. "And you, Jack Fortune. What of you? What did you search for? And what did you find?"

Jack jumped. He hadn't expected that. The Abbot looked steadily at him, waiting for an answer.

"I suppose… I found my uncle," he said slowly. "I didn't really know him before. He never said much when he came to stay with Aunt Constance. Mind you, that's not surprising – he probably couldn't get a word in edgeways. But I know him now. He's brave – really brave. And he wants to do good things. It doesn't always come out right, but he tries his best." He thought for a bit more, and then took a deep breath. "And I found my father as well. I didn't even know I was looking for him, but I was. I think I always have been, in a way. I never knew him before, but now I feel as if I do. And that's thanks to Uncle Edmund."

Uncle Edmund stared in astonishment. "Why, Jack!" he said. "Good Heavens! I mean – good Lord!"

Jack shrugged, embarrassed. He couldn't imagine that he would ever have said such things, anywhere else

but in this little room, in front of this wise old man –
but he knew they were true. The Abbot smiled, and Jack
felt suddenly that everything was going to be all right.

This was the moment. If he was to make his request,
it must be now.

He stood up, went over to the Abbot and knelt down
in front of him.

"Sir," he said, swallowing hard. "I... I have something
to ask. A favour. A big one. It's not for me – it's for
Uncle Edmund. He's lost his dream – you know that.
It wasn't his fault, not at all, and I want to find it again
for him."

Uncle Edmund looked taken aback, and Thondup
stared at Jack in surprise. The Abbot's head was tilted
to one side, considering. He looked like a bright-eyed
bird.

"If it exists, I want to find the hidden valley. I want...
I would like... I wish to ask, sir, if I may go on, and
search for it on Mount Zemu." Ignoring the intake of
breath from all around the room, he hurried on. "I
know the mountain is holy, sir – I know that – but I
can't see why the god would mind if it was just me and
I was very careful. It's not for me: it's for my uncle, and
I won't do any damage." He remembered the phrase
his uncle had used to the Maharaja, it now seemed so
long ago. "I will tread lightly, sir. I will tread lightly on
the land, I promise. Only please let me go – please!"

Was it enough? Had he managed to find the right words? Would the Abbot understand?

The Abbot gazed at him. Though his eyes were dark, there was a light in them, and Jack dared to hope.

"The valley exists. There is a path. But no man is allowed in this place, Jack Fortune."

Terrified that he might cry, Jack bit the edge of his hand hard. But the Abbot was still speaking.

"However, you are a boy – not a man – and I think you are pure of heart. I believe that Zemu may permit it." Jack gasped – was it possible? Was the Abbot really going to let him go? But before he could say a word, the Abbot held up a hand to stop him – and now he was looking stern.

"There are two…" he turned and murmured something to Thondup, who supplied the word he needed. "Yes, two conditions. One is that you must go alone. The other is this. If Zemu gives you this great gift, you must give him something in return. What shall it be?"

Jack waited, puzzled. What did he mean? What could Jack possibly have that would be of any interest to Zemu?

Thondup said quickly, "Be careful, Jack. This is dangerous. Do not offer anything that you cannot afford to lose."

Then Uncle Edmund, clearly very agitated, spoke: "Jack, I absolutely forbid this. The mountain is dangerous – we *know* that. Look at what has already happened! You can't possibly go off by yourself – if anything happened to you, your Aunt Constance would never forgive me – and indeed, I would not forgive myself!"

But Jack wasn't listening. His mind was racing. What did he have? What could he give?

And then he knew.

"What I take from the mountain, I'll give back. If I find the flower, I'll make the monastery a gift to take its place. I promise."

The Abbot gazed into Jack's eyes. Then he nodded. "Agreed. It shall be so. You will leave in the morning."

So it was settled. Jack had got his way. He was going to find the blue rhododendron!

CHAPTER FOURTEEN

The Hidden Valley

The next morning, Jack woke early, with a vague sense that something was wrong. It wasn't long before he remembered what it was. He thought about what had happened after they'd met the Abbot the day before. Thondup had pleaded with him.

"What you have seen so far will be as *nothing* compared to what it will be like out there." He gestured towards the mountain behind the monastery. "The snow will be treacherous. The cold will turn your breath to ice as it leaves your mouth. You may think you are walking on solid ground, and all of a sudden, *crash*! You will fall into a bottomless ravine. There will be precipices, cliffs – more avalanches, perhaps. The danger you have experienced so far will be as nothing compared to what lies ahead!"

CHAPTER FOURTEEN

"Oh, good Heavens!" said Uncle Edmund faintly. "Jack, I absolutely forbid it! The thought of you all alone – no, no, it just won't do."

Jack sighed. His uncle seemed to have very little faith in him.

"I *have* seen snow before, you know," he pointed out. "Of course I'll be careful – but the Abbot said there was a path, so it surely won't be *that* difficult. Don't worry – I'll be back in no time. I'll find the blue rhododendron, and then all our troubles will be over!"

Now though, in the cold grey light of morning, it felt more as if his troubles were just beginning.

But he told himself firmly that he had a job to do, so he'd better get on and do it. After breakfast, he put on Mr Inchmore's sheepskin coat and slipped Sonam's turquoise stone into the pocket. Perhaps it would bring him luck. As he wrapped round his neck the scarf that Sarah Puddy had given him, he thought about Will. If only he was here now, and they were setting off together! It would have been so much more fun. He sighed.

All the inhabitants of the monastery had gathered to see him on his way. They all seemed very subdued. Some of the older monks looked at him anxiously and murmured what sounded like prayers. The younger ones, catching the mood, looked at him with large, sorrowful eyes. They all looked so dismal that it was really quite depressing, and suddenly Jack couldn't wait to get away.

Thondup looked desperately worried, and Uncle Edmund made one last attempt to get him to change his mind.

"Jack, I know you are doing this for me, and don't think I don't appreciate it. But… well, what I want to say is… ahem! How best to put it? Scientifically, it's true I haven't gained what I hoped to from this trip. But in other ways, I have gained far more than I could ever, ever have imagined. I… I don't suppose now that I will ever have a son. But – in short – were I to be so fortunate… why then I could wish nothing better than to have one rather like you. *Exactly* like you, in fact. And it would sadden me very greatly if, having found… yourself… I were then to lose you. So I will ask you one more time – *please* do not do this. You are worth *far* more to me than any flower, no matter how beautiful or how rare."

Jack was horrified. His uncle looked as if he was about to burst into tears! "Look, Uncle," he said kindly, "all I'm doing is going for a little walk in the snow. I'll be extremely careful, and I'll be back before you know it. So please stop worrying and, um, cheer up."

He stuck his hand out – but, with a funny sort of harrumphing noise, Uncle Edmund hugged him, almost losing his balance in the process.

CHAPTER FOURTEEN

Then it was time to say goodbye to Thondup. Jack sighed, ready for another lecture.

But he didn't get it. Instead, Thondup bowed slightly, his hands together, and then said quietly, "You have all the courage you need within you. Just remember to look for it. Watch where you put your feet and come back safely."

The monks gave him bread and a couple of handfuls of dried apricots. He stowed the food in his father's bag, along with a few seed boxes, his knife and his father's drawing book and paints.

Then there was nothing left to do and it was time to go.

He hoped Thondup was right. He hoped that, when he needed it, his courage would be there, ready and waiting.

The Abbot took him to the gateway which opened onto the mountain.

"There is the path," he said, smiling encouragingly. "If Zemu is willing, your way will be clear to you."

"And what if he isn't willing?" asked Jack.

The Abbot beamed helpfully. "Oh, he will make that quite clear."

Very encouraging, thought Jack. And how, exactly, would Zemu make his will clear? Perhaps he'd send another avalanche. He remembered the tumbling scree and flying boulders of the night they had spent camped on the open mountain, and shuddered. Still, no use to think about that. It was too late to back out now.

The path climbed quickly, and before long he reached the snowline. He felt much better now he was on his way, and, in a sudden burst of cheerfulness, he thought how incredibly lucky he was to be up here on top of the world, instead of being shut up in a dreary classroom or in his aunt's stifling parlour. Zemu was looking very beautiful. The sky glowed red and gold, tinting the snow with shades of rose and apricot. He wound his scarf tightly round his face, to capture the warmth of his breath. What was it Sarah used to say? Oh yes, that was it: "Red sky at night, shepherd's delight; red sky in the morning, shepherd's warning…" Hm. Well, that was in England. It probably didn't work like that over here.

He started to whistle a cheery tune, but his voice sounded thin and small, lost in the enormity of the mountains. Perhaps Zemu didn't like whistling. Perhaps it was disrespectful. "Sorry," he muttered. "Beg your pardon."

The path was steep now. His legs began to ache, and it became more difficult to get his breath. Soon the sun was high in the sky, and the snow sparkled so brightly that it dazzled his eyes. It was getting deeper. It was powdery and inviting, and at first he kicked it so it exploded in little flurries. But it wasn't so much fun without someone like Will Puddy to aim at, and anyway he found it made him out of breath, so in the end he just trudged onward. The path was clearly marked with posts and prayer flags at intervals.

After an hour or so, he stopped for a rest. The monastery was far below, and for a little while he watched the little black dots that must have been the monks moving around in the courtyard. He'd liked the monks. They were serious and fun at the same time.

He turned away and carried on, wondering how much farther it would be. It was all going well so far. In fact, he was beginning to wonder what all the fuss had been about. You just had to keep putting one foot after the other. He just hoped the stories were true, and the blue rhododendron would be there at the end of it.

Then, suddenly, the path stopped dead. It didn't have much choice, because it had reached a ravine.

There was a bridge. But it wasn't an ordinary bridge. This bridge was made of ice.

Smooth, glistening, slippery ice.

Jack gazed at it in dismay. How on earth was he to get across *that*?

His eyes ran over it, hoping against hope that the ice might be just a coating over a normal bridge. But no. There were no posts, no signs of anything made by man. This was solid ice, pure and simple. He guessed that in the winter the whole ravine had been filled up with snow and ice, and now this was all that was left.

He approached the ravine very, very carefully, and peered over the edge. The bottom was littered with jagged rocks, jutting cruelly out of a coverlet of snow. If you fell down there, it wouldn't be a soft landing.

"Is this a joke?" he muttered to the god. "Because if it is, I don't think myself that it's very funny."

The wind echoed around the mountain tops. It sounded like mocking laughter.

He could see the bright flags marking the path on the other side. He was meant to go across – there was no doubt about it. He was getting very, very cold; there was no doubt about that either. He stamped his feet and tucked his gloved hands under his arms and tried to think .

What on earth – or on ice – was he to do?

He went back to the edge of the bridge again. It was about six strides across, at a guess – but of course you wouldn't be able to stride, not on a surface as smooth and slippery as glass. You'd only have to make one tiny slip, and then… his eyes travelled down to the waiting rocks. He felt the familiar churning sensation again, the same one he'd felt looking down at the River Dalpo, and up at the perpendicular ladder.

The truth hit him like a hammer. He simply couldn't do it. Not him, not stupid Jack Fortune, utterly useless explorer with a fear of heights. He'd tried – nobody could say he hadn't – but he would just have to admit that, after all his brave words, he'd failed. He'd let Uncle Edmund down. He'd just have to go back and tell him so.

Then he seemed to hear Thondup's voice. "You have all the courage you need within you. Just remember to look for it…"

He shivered, and not just because of the cold. He couldn't go across, but he couldn't give up either. He couldn't go back and say he'd failed because it had got too difficult – he just couldn't. He peered at the bridge again. It was so narrow – hardly wider than a wall.

A wall – that was it. That was the key. He closed his eyes. Back in Little Stinchcombe, Mr Prout had an orchard. It had the best apples in the village – all the boys knew it. They also knew it was surrounded by a high wall. All you had to do was clamber up onto the wall and edge along the top, and in no time at all those delicious apples were yours for the picking.

Jack opened his eyes and blinked, almost surprised to see the harsh glare of snow instead of the soft green of an English summer. He kept the picture in his head. All he had to do, he told himself fiercely, was imagine that the ice bridge was Mr Prout's wall. He crouched in the snow at the edge of the ravine, and inched forward till he was sitting astride the bridge. Then he began to work his way forward, thinking about apples.

Before long he had reached the middle. Feeling cautiously pleased with himself, he stopped for a rest and looked around.

He should have known better.

There were no trees, and this wasn't Mr Prout's wall. The mountains were spinning wildly round his head, there was a dizzying drop below and he felt sure he was about to slip. He grabbed hold of the bridge, wrapped himself round it and held on for dear life.

He tried to think. What had he done when he'd been on the ladder? He heard again Thondup's voice: *Think only about your breathing…* He thought about Uncle Edmund. He thought about Thondup and the Maharaja. He thought about Aunt Constance, and how good it would be to have something to be proud of next time he saw her. Then he thought about the Dewan, and how he'd tried to destroy Uncle Edmund's dream – and that did it. If he didn't get to the valley, the Dewan would have won.

Carefully, making no sudden movements, Jack uncurled and sat up. He began to breathe slowly and deeply, concentrating on that and nothing else. Finally, when he was sure he was ready, he began to shuffle forward again, very slowly and carefully, till at last he reached the other side.

CHAPTER FOURTEEN

He'd done it!

After that, the rest was easy. The path began to wind down into a gulley. The sides grew steeper, but the god or some of his earthly helpers had kindly carved out steps in the rock, and all Jack had to do was run down them into a narrow valley.

Because of the way the valley was positioned, it was protected from the winds that whipped round the mountain. The air was still cold, but it was very much milder than on the outside. Jack looked round in wonder. It was similar to the other valley, the one Sonam had led them to, but it was even more beautiful. A shallow stream ran through it, and ferns, pink and purple primulas, slender yellow irises and brilliant turquoise poppies grew on the banks. The craggy slopes were covered with trees – and such trees! Jack caught his breath in astonishment. There were more species of rhododendron than he had seen in the whole of Hakkim. The flowers ranged from delicate lemon bells to huge scarlet globes. They were every colour, size and shape you could possibly imagine. They were stunning.

If only Uncle Edmund could have been there to see! Then, with a start, Jack remembered what he had come for, and set off in search of the most important colour of all.

There was so much colour he was almost dizzy with it. There was flame red, apricot, lilac, crimson, palest rose pink, lemon yellow and creamy white. He wanted to paint all of it, but he knew he didn't have time. He mustn't be out on the mountain tonight – he had no camping gear, and even if he did, he would be lucky to survive the bitter cold that would descend with darkness.

He pulled himself together and walked slowly along beside the stream, scanning the slopes from side to side, desperate for a glimpse of blue.

"It's got to be here," he muttered to himself. "It's just got to be!"

He wouldn't dare contemplate the thought that it might after all be just a story, a travellers' tale, and that, even after all this, he might have to return with nothing.

Then he heard a new sound, a rushing, splashing sound. And there, just around the next bend, was a waterfall. At its base was a pool – and round the pool were rhododendron bushes, whose flowers were not red, not yellow, not pink, not white – but the most beautiful blue: like little pieces of heaven.

For a moment, Jack just stood there, spellbound. Then a huge grin spread from ear to ear.

"It's here, Uncle," he whispered. "The blue rhododendron! It really is!"

But there was no time to stand and stare. He had to work fast. First, he pulled out his sketchbook and paints. He didn't have much time, so he just did quick sketches, of the whole truss, of each individual floret, of the way the leaves grew on the branch, of the shape of the whole bush. Then he painted little squares of blue, experimenting with different mixes and intensities till he had, as near as possible, exactly the right shade.

Next, he cut some of the flowers and leaves, pressed them between plant papers and stowed them carefully in his bag. He knew that shoots without any flowers on them were the best ones for growing new plants, so he found some of those too, and wrapped them in damp moss so they wouldn't dry out. Finally, he cut a few whole flowers and placed them at the top of the bag, blessing his father for having had such a roomy one. The flowers might get crushed, but if they didn't, he would love to see his uncle's face when he laid eyes on them.

He knew he should head back to the abbey now, but having come so far to find this place he felt reluctant to leave. He wondered if Zemu was watching. Perhaps he should do something to show his respect. He put his hands together and bowed very deeply, as he'd seen so many people do since he'd come to India.

He looked round, trying to imprint the place on his memory; the rich deep green of the trees, the bright, frothy flowers, the clear, ice-cold water of the stream… and then he noticed something. Up at the top of the waterfall, behind the thin sparkling sheet of water, there was a darkness. He knew what it was instantly. It was a cave – a *secret* cave! And everyone knew what secret caves contained – treasure!

It was just too tempting. Telling himself it would only take a few minutes, he began to scramble up the slope.

The waterfall was like a glimmering curtain in front of the entrance. Behind it there was a ledge, and then a short tunnel before the cave opened out. It took a moment or two for Jack's eyes to adjust to the darkness, but gradually he could see that the cave was not empty.

There were things in it – lots of things! His excitement grew. The dim shapes looked like boxes and sacks. He felt his way farther in. A little daylight filtered in from outside, and he saw the dull gleam of something metallic – a clasp, on what his hands told him was quite certainly a wooden chest.

He tried the lid. With only a slight creak, it opened. He hesitated. Who could tell what was inside? It could be anything. Perhaps it wasn't treasure after all. He shivered, his imagination running riot. It could be a body! He sniffed the air. Nothing. Tentatively, he reached inside – and felt something hard and cold, something which jingled as he pulled it out and flashed as he turned it towards the light. It was a necklace, gold and set with coloured stones. Unbelievable! It really was a treasure chest! He dropped it back in and rummaged about for something else. He came up with another necklace. This one gleamed white – it was made of pearls.

He left the chest and made his way over to one of the sacks. These felt different, as if they were full of sand, and there was a smell that he couldn't quite place. He stuck his finger in and licked it cautiously.

It was salt.

Salt and jewels. But why? What were they doing here? Could it be something to do with the monastery?

Suddenly, what light there had been was extinguished. Something – somebody – was blocking the entrance. Instinctively, Jack scooped up two handfuls of salt and crouched down. Whoever it was wouldn't be able to see him in this dark – and whoever it was, unless he was a monk, had no right to be here.

He stayed absolutely still, his heart pounding. Then the newcomer spoke – in English. And although Jack had only heard it once before, he recognized the voice immediately. It was deep, resentful and hostile – and it belonged to the Dewan.

Jack didn't bother to wonder what it all meant or how he'd got here. All that mattered was that he *was* here, he was the enemy and he was blocking off Jack's way out.

"I know you are here, English boy. Come – I will help you. We must return to Dilphut, it grows late.

What… what is this place? Come over here – come to me…"

He moved, and a ray of light found its way in and struck a gleam off something the Dewan held in his hand. It was a *kukri*, a vicious, curved knife. Jack was suddenly very still. The Dewan was not here to help. Well, Jack had not expected that. But he hadn't imagined that he was here to kill.

More light trickled in. The Dewan was moving farther into the cave. Jack had an advantage. The Dewan had only just come into the cave – his eyes wouldn't be used to the dark. Jack stood up very quietly and began to edge towards the entrance. He was still for a moment, looking around.

"Where are you?" said the Dewan sharply. "I saw you enter. I know you are here – do not think to hide."

Jack kept moving. But he needed the Dewan to move too, so that he could get to the entrance.

"It's yours, isn't it?" he said, finding his voice. "All this stuff in here. Why do you keep it here – what's it for?"

The Dewan turned sharply, and edged his way towards Jack. "You British," he snarled, "always with your noses into everything. You have no right to be here, and one day—"

He was close enough now. Jack threw the salt in his face, praying he wouldn't miss. Startled, the Dewan cried out in pain, and his knife clattered to the floor of the cave as he dropped it to clutch his face with his hands. Jack made a dash for the entrance, rolled, bumped and slithered his way down the slope and paused.

He knew he was in terrible danger. The salt would keep the Dewan blinded for a few minutes, but as soon as he could see again, he'd be after him. Jack thought quickly. Perhaps he could hide? But he knew the Dewan wouldn't leave the valley without him. Jack knew his secret. And the Dewan must know the valley much better than Jack did. No, he was younger and fitter – his best bet was to run.

He reached the steps that led out of the valley and leapt up them. But the steps were steep, each breath tore its way painfully out of his chest and his legs began to feel weak. Behind him he could hear the Dewan, stumbling and cursing. Jack forced himself to keep going. If he was struggling, with any luck the Dewan with all his bulk would be doing even worse.

When the steps came to an end, there was still the steep slope leading up to the ice bridge. He ran on, forcing one foot after another. And all the time, the thought of the ice bridge, slender and lethal, was leaking into his mind.

It had been almost impossibly difficult when he'd had all the time in the world. How was he going to manage it with a knife-wielding maniac behind him? He felt a stinging in his eyes, and he didn't know whether it was from sweat or tears. It was all going to be for nothing. He'd end up at the bottom of the ravine and no one would ever know.

No. He had the blue rhododendron. Zemu was on his side. He was not going to give up.

When he reached the bridge, Jack sank to his knees in the snow, closed his eyes and began to pray. He reminded the god that he had respected the mountain and the valley. He pointed out that he was perfectly prepared to fulfil his side of the bargain and make the promised gift – but he was going to need a little help.

Nothing happened.

Exhausted, he opened his eyes and looked at the bridge. It glittered in the sunlight, cruel and beautiful. He had to cross it, and it looked as if he was on his own.

Then, at the other side of the bridge, he saw something. What was it? It was like a tall, dark shadow. He narrowed his eyes, not certain if the dazzling sunshine reflecting from the snow was deceiving him. Was it one of the monks? He really couldn't see it clearly. He blinked. Was it looking at him? Tentatively, he stretched out his arms. The shadowy shape stretched its arms out too. Suddenly, Jack had the sense that it was perfectly safe to walk across the ice bridge, that nothing would harm him. There was no need to be afraid. All he had to do was put one foot in front of the other…

As if in a dream, he set off. It was as simple as if he was walking along the familiar path that led up to Aunt Constance's door. He was quite sure that he would reach the other side, and he would be safe.

And so it was.

Having reached the other side, he turned slowly. He felt as if he was in a golden bubble, somehow outside himself.

The Dewan was about to step onto the bridge. He was looking at it warily, but he had no choice. Jack knew his secret, and he couldn't be allowed to get away.

Jack looked at the bridge. There was something subtly different about it and, as he stared, he realized what it was. The sun had been shining all day. Drops of water were trickling down its sides; the surface was beginning to melt.

Suddenly, Jack knew what was going to happen. The Dewan was far heavier than Jack. The bridge had borne Jack's weight, but…

"No!" Jack shouted. "Don't step onto the bridge – it'll give way! DON'T!"

The Dewan looked across at him and scowled, obviously thinking Jack was trying to trick him. Stretching his arms out for balance, he began to come across. Jack began to back away – and found himself being lifted into the air by strong arms.

He saw a look of astonishment in the Dewan's face. The man hesitated – and then there came a loud crack. He looked backwards and forwards in terror, panicking as it dawned on him what was going to happen. There was another crack, and yet another. The Dewan flailed wildly, and Jack watched in horror. But there was nothing he could do. The bridge splintered, and with a scream that echoed round the peaks of Zemu, the Dewan hurtled down into the ravine and lay still, a crumpled, doll-like figure, broken by the rocks.

Jack closed his eyes and fainted.

CHAPTER FIFTEEN

The Gift

The voice seemed to come from somewhere far, far away. Jack stirred. Where was he? What had happened? There had been a figure, a shadow creature... he seemed to see it, turning to wave at him, and then clouds and mist wrapped round it and it was hidden. He felt a sharp sense of loss, and then he realized that his uncle was speaking.

"Surely he should be awake by now? It's been hours since we found him. Oh, I shall never forgive myself if he has come to harm – never, not in this world or the next..."

Jack's eyelids fluttered open, and Uncle Edmund's face appeared above him.

"Jack! Oh, thank goodness!"

Jack smiled vaguely. Something had happened. Something important...

A series of pictures came to him, jostling each other to get to the front of the queue, and all at once he was wide awake. He struggled up onto his elbows. "Uncle! My father's bag – did you find it?"

"Thondup, Champa, look, he's all right! You *are* all right, aren't you?" demanded his uncle anxiously. "No aches and pains?"

"Yes, I'm fine – really fine! But uncle – the bag!"

His uncle smiled a huge and joyous smile. "Oh yes, Jack, we did find the bag. And everything in it is safe. That beautiful, beautiful flower... and you must tell me everything. But all in good time, my dear boy, all in good time. *You* are the most important thing."

Jack lay back on his cushions. Some of the other pictures were clamouring for his attention, and he frowned, trying to remember. There had been the cave, and the Dewan, and a bridge made of ice...

His eyes widened in horror. "The Dewan," he said. "I think he's dead!"

There was a shocked silence. Then Thondup leant forward.

"The Dewan?" he said. "What has he to do with this? All we know is that the bell rang at the gate to the monastery, and there you were, curled up in the snow, unconscious but safe. Who brought you here, Jack? Do you have any idea?"

"It must have been the guardian," said Jack slowly. "He was tall and... and... you remember the story about the *metoh-kangmi*, Thondup – the guardians? That if you see one you will witness a death? I did see one, and there *was* a death..."

He told them everything. At the end, Thondup looked at Champa, who nodded.

"He must have been the stranger who came to the monastery earlier," said Champa, understanding dawning on his face. "I will go and see the Abbot. If this man is truly dead, we will leave him to a sky burial. But perhaps he is only injured. We must go and search for him..."

"A sky burial? What's that?" asked Uncle Edmund after Champa had hurried off.

"It means that when a person dies, his body is given back to the mountain, and the birds pick clean his bones," explained Thondup.

Jack and his uncle looked at each other, horrified. They knew so little about this country. Its customs were so very different from their own.

But it turned out that neither a sky burial nor any other kind was necessary. The Dewan was badly injured, and suffering from the effects of exposure, but he was not dead. The monks brought him back to Dilphut and nursed him. It would take time, but eventually he would recover – and then he would have to explain himself.

He was no longer a threat, and Jack had other things to think about. He owed Zemu a gift. In fact, he thought, he owed him one twice over: once for the flower, as he had promised the Abbot, and once for his life. Without the help of the guardian, the Dewan would have caught him. And the guardian had only appeared after he had prayed to Zemu.

He asked the monks for a piece of silk. He was going to make a prayer flag. It would be a very special prayer flag. It would not have words on it, but a picture.

He used every bit of skill he'd accumulated over the last few months to make it the best picture he had ever done. He wanted to imbue it with both the stern, icy mystery of the mountains that last for ever, and the fragile beauty of a flower that lasts for only a few days. So in the background were the snowy peaks of Zemu, while in the foreground a waterfall sparkled beside a rhododendron – whose flowers, of course, were a clear and heavenly blue. And, somewhere in between, there was a shadowy figure, whose eyes held all the tenderness of a parent bending over a sleeping child.

When he'd finished, he presented it to the Abbot. The old man spread it out carefully and gazed at it for a long time. His old eyes glittered as he looked at Jack, and he nodded.

"Your picture will have a special place on the mountain. It speaks of the beauty of our country, and also of its strength. The winds will breathe its message to every corner of the world. You have done well, Jack Fortune. The god will be pleased."

Jack bowed his head. "I hope so," he said.

They stayed at the monastery for another two weeks. Uncle Edmund wanted to learn as much as he could about the uses the monks made of plants and herbs, and they all welcomed the chance to rest and build up their strength ready for the journey back. Uncle Edmund would have to be carried; it would be many weeks before his leg would be completely mended. He was unhappy about this, concerned at the extra burden he would put on the porters, but they assured him that his weight was no more than a feather's and constructed, under Thondup's direction, a sort of sedan chair, so that he could be carried sitting up.

When the Dewan regained consciousness, Thondup and the Abbot interviewed him together.

"He has been driven by greed," Thondup told Uncle Edmund and Jack afterwards. "His hatred of the British was real. But his main concern was that, with their passion for trade, they would step into what he believed to be his territory. For years he has been the one who controlled trade in Hakkim. My father trusted him, and he has used the power that gave him to steal and extort from the people. He has built up a great treasure, and this was what you found in the cave." He was silent for a moment, his face cold and remote. "He will answer for this to my father."

Jack felt a chill. "What will happen to him?" he asked.

"That is not your concern," said Thondup.

There was an awkward silence, and then Uncle Edmund said, "But I still don't quite see why he was so set against our own expedition." He looked a little embarrassed. "After all, your father specifically forbade us from going to Mount Zemu; surely there was very little danger of us discovering his secret?"

Thondup smiled. "The British are not known for doing what they are told. He could not risk it. And also, if *your* expedition ended in failure, his hope was that others would see the danger and stay away."

"Ah yes," said Uncle Edmund, nodding wisely, "I see."

Jack shuddered, remembering the moment when the Dewan's knife had glinted in the cave. Death had been very close.

He had not forgotten his promise to tell the Maharaja the story of their journey, and he was eager to see Mr Inchmore and tell him all about their adventures.

But then it would be time to go home. And he was looking forward to that too.

CHAPTER SIXTEEN

Epilogue

"So this is it, Jack," said Uncle Edmund nervously. "Somerset House, the headquarters of the Royal Society. Well – let us be bold!"

He lifted the heavy brass knocker and let it drop against the door. It swung open, and a uniformed footman appeared.

"Mr Edmund Pascoe and Master Jack Fortune," announced Uncle Edmund. "Here to see the President of the Society – Sir Joseph Banks."

The footman bowed. "Sir Joseph is expecting you, sir. Please follow me."

They walked along marble corridors and into a great hall. Jack stared. It wasn't the best room he had ever seen – that was still the Maharaja's – but it was certainly the grandest. Golden chandeliers hung from the lofty ceiling, and portraits lined the walls.

At the front, a tall, bulky man stood waiting for them. He wore a grey wig, and his dark eyes were alert and interested. Facing him were long seats filled with men and women who turned towards Jack and his uncle as the double doors opened and they were announced. As they walked up to the front, Jack caught sight of Aunt Constance. She smiled and waved at them, and dabbed delicately beneath her eyes with a small scrap of lace. Goodness, thought Jack, anyone would think she was proud of us!

Sir Joseph smiled warmly at them and began to speak.

"Members and honoured guests of the Royal Society! May I present to you, fresh from their expedition to the remote valleys and mountains of the Himalayas, Mr Edmund Pascoe and Master Jack Fortune, who have brought us, among other delights, *Rhododendron floracelestia*, the remarkable and utterly exquisite blue rhododendron which has taken the horticultural world by storm."

As the audience clapped and cheered, Jack glanced at his uncle in surprise. "*Floracelestia*?" he whispered, stumbling over the long Latin word. "I thought you were going to call it *pascoensis*?"

Uncle Edmund shook his head. "I changed my mind. I came to understand that I don't need to have a plant named after me – or at least not this plant. After all, it was you who found it. I *was* going to call it after you. And then I thought that – well, in all the circumstances, you might think that 'heavenly blue' is more fitting. It will remind us... of so much."

Jack smiled. "It's perfect!" he whispered.

Then he realized that Sir Joseph was speaking to them both. "On behalf of His Majesty King George, the Royal Society and the botanical gardens of Kew, I congratulate you. May this be only the first of many such journeys! And now, will you tell us about your expedition?"

"Of course," beamed Uncle Edmund. "Well, where to begin..."

The audience listened, enthralled – especially when Jack took over the story and told them about the Dewan and the guardian. "It was huge!" he said. "Huge!"

Some of the ladies gasped, and Aunt Constance nodded proudly. "He was always such a good, brave boy," she said fondly.

Finally, when they had finished, Sir Joseph held out his arms and declared, in a ringing voice: "Ladies and gentleman, I give you Fortune and Pascoe – plant hunters to the King!"

Afterword

The Plant Hunters

There are lots of books about famous explorers who sailed the seas looking for new countries – Christopher Columbus, Sir Walter Raleigh, John Cabot, to name just a few. They were great adventurers: just imagine setting off across the ocean in a small wooden ship, not knowing what you would find on the other side – or even if there *was* another side! (Map-makers, when they came to the end of what they knew, would simply write: *Here be dragons*.) And still today, there are people who go off in search of the last frontier – in the desert, in the jungle, in the Arctic regions.

Less well known is another group of adventurers who, over the centuries, have also wandered far and wide, risking their lives (and sometimes losing them) on the highest mountains, the deepest rivers and in the thickest forests.

What were they searching for, these people? Not for precious metals or jewels, not for new territory, not to set new records for the longest trek or the steepest climb. No. They were looking for – plants.

Very few of the trees, flowers and shrubs which grow in British gardens actually originated in this country. Many plants, like roses, lilies and horse chestnut (conker) trees, come from North America and Asia. They were brought here by plant hunters, who undertook dangerous journeys into remote parts of the world, little known to people in the West, in search of beautiful, and often useful, new plants – for which British gardeners would pay a great deal of money.

Sir Joseph Banks

The end of the eighteenth century, when George III was on the throne, was a time of change. All sorts of exciting things were happening, particularly in science. For example, William Herschel and his sister Caroline were building powerful new telescopes with which to explore the night sky, and Humphry Davy was soon to invent the Davy Lamp, which would save many miners' lives – before then, lamps underground had caused many explosions when they ignited dangerous gases. In France, the Montgolfier brothers were eagerly experimenting with hot-air balloons – people were thrilled at the idea that they might be able to fly above the surface of the earth! A scientist called Luigi Galvani noticed that electricity could apparently make dead animals move – and some years later, eighteen year-old Mary Shelley, wondering where all these scientific developments might lead, wrote a book called *Frankenstein*, about a scientist who gives life to a creature which is half-man, half-monster.

At the centre of all this excitement and discovery was a man called Sir Joseph Banks. As a boy, Banks became fascinated by botany, the study of plants. When he grew up, instead of going on a Grand Tour of Europe, which was what most wealthy young men did, he took a post as a naturalist on board a ship surveying the remote coastline of Labrador and Newfoundland. A couple of years later, he joined Captain Cook in his expedition to the South Seas, which was to travel all round the world, exploring on the way the scarcely known territories of Tahiti, New Zealand and Australia.

Banks had an absolutely marvellous time, exploring, collecting plant specimens and meeting all sorts of interesting people. When he came back, everyone – including King George – was fascinated by the stories he had to tell. The King had a beautiful garden at Kew, just outside London. Banks helped him to make it into one of the most important botanical gardens in the world, sending plant hunters all over the globe in search of exciting new flowers, trees and plants with which to fill it.

He also became President of the Royal Society. This was, and still is, a society which only the very best scientists are asked to join. Banks encouraged people like the Herschels and Davy by giving them grants of money so that they could carry on with their work.

This is the background to *Jack Fortune and the Search for the Hidden Valley*, in which Jack, whose ambition is to be an explorer, sets off on an expedition to the Himalayas with his uncle Edmund Pascoe. Sir Joseph Banks is Edmund's hero; he hopes that if his trip is successful, Sir Joseph will notice him – and with luck, employ him!